NEVER FIND ANOTHER YOU

TRINITY LAKES ROMANCE
BOOK ONE

NARELLE ATKINS

Never Find Another You

1st edition 2023 — Narelle Atkins

Copyright © 2023 by Narelle Atkins

Narelle Atkins

PO BOX 512

Jamison Centre ACT 2614

AUSTRALIA

www.narelleatkins.com

This book is a work of fiction. Any resemblance to actual events or persons, living or dead, is coincidental.

Cover Art by Melissa Dalley

Never Find Another You/Narelle Atkins. —1st ed.

ISBN: 1-922915-04-1

ISBN-13: 978-1-922915-04-7

❀ Created with Vellum

CHAPTER ONE

Who needed the stress from a busy and complicated big city career when they could work beside a beautiful lake? Hannah Gilbertson stood on the rowing club veranda, leaning her elbows on the wooden railing, and her coffee mug warming her hands. Two white swans glided through the gentle swell beside the Lake Wainscott dock.

Trinity Lakes may only be a sleepy, small Eastern Washington town close to the mountains, but it was her hometown. The place where she'd grown up, the place where she'd trained to achieve a college sports scholarship, and the only place she wanted to call home.

Hannah inhaled the rich coffee aroma swirling in the steam from her mug. Her morning latte courtesy of her sister's coffee cart, and hand delivered by their grandma.

Grandma joined her on the veranda and sat on a weather-worn wooden bench. "Nice morning on the lake."

Hannah nodded. "It's warm for late February. Spring's here early."

"I hope so." Grandma stretched in her seat, her small frame

hidden inside a bulky purple velour tracksuit. "My old bones ache when it's cold."

Hannah chuckled. Her seventy-something grandma was a live wire who rarely sat for longer than a few minutes. "You can count down the days until March arrives."

"I'll be gardening in your mother's yard. There's too much planting and yard work to do at this time of year."

"I know, right?" She had a long list of maintenance jobs to finish before the warmer weather brought more tourists to the lake. "My job list for today is long."

Grandma sipped tea from her thermos. "One day you can retire and enjoy these sunny mornings with a light breeze and birdsong for company."

Hannah laughed. "I'm only halfway to fifty. Retirement and bird watching is way off in the future."

"You could retire early, or borrow my binoculars and watch the birds during your breaks."

"Who has time for that?"

"People make time. I heard you're working through lunch most days."

She shrugged off the concern in Grandma's voice. "I like eating at my desk." When the clubhouse bustled with talkative seniors at lunchtime, she'd escape to her office for peace and quiet and a can't-stop-turning-the-page book.

"At least Becky and I can keep you supplied with good coffee." Grandma stood. "My morning exercise is good for me."

"It sure is, and I appreciate you." Grandma had their coffee routine all figured out. She collected Hannah's favorite mug and matching lid, walked across the road to Becky's coffee cart and stopped for a chat, then returned with a hot mug of coffee for Hannah's morning break.

Hannah sipped her latte. "I'd rather be out on the water rowing or kayaking than working indoors, but I've got bills to pay." Her membership business model for the community-oriented rowing club, combined with the additional tourism income in peak seasons, kept the club in the black and provided Hannah with a modest salary. "What's on your schedule for today?"

Grandma sighed. "Avoiding your mother. She's in a mood, and I'm not sure why."

"I'm sorry." Mom was difficult at the best of times, and downright impossible at her worst.

"There's no reason to apologize."

"My guest room is yours, if you need it."

"No way." Grandma shook her head, her pink tipped gray curls bobbing around her sweet face. "Your siblings would never forgive me for stealing your spare room and their escape plan from your mother."

"Good point." Dan, her older brother, and Leanna, her youngest sister, used her downstairs guest room if they didn't stay with Mom. Becky had moved into the second bedroom when she'd quit college. Their father had claimed the third bedroom as his own by filling it with stuff he might need when he visited. Traveling light was not in her father's vocabulary.

"I'll survive your mother, my dear girl. She'll calm down. Eventually."

"You have more patience than me." Grandma was a survivor. Since Grandpa passed away seven years ago, she'd moved in with Mom after Hannah had graduated high school and started her business degree in Boston.

"I need to finish my crochet project before class tomorrow," Grandma said.

"Is this the colorful throw you've been talking about?"

"It sure is. A few hours of work this afternoon will finish it."

"Good for you, Grandma." The Village Shoppes Emporium off Main Street was known for their quaint stores and entrepreneurial vendors who offered popular community classes. That part of town drew the crowds year-round. Exploring the barn-like building was an enchanting experience, like walking onto a charming small-town movie set.

Hannah drained her coffee cup. "Break time is over. I've got muddy showers and restrooms to clean before the tiler arrives."

Grandma's eyes lit up. "Ooh, you're talking about the Aussie guy who's new to town?"

"Yeah. His boss said he'll be here sometime this morning to give me a quote." Sometime could be anywhere between eight and twelve. Not helpful when she'd had the high school rowing team training here before school this morning.

"I've heard he's a nice-looking young man, and your age, too."

"Grandma, please stop. You're starting to sound like Mom—"

"I've got better taste than your mother. There's no comparison."

"Really?" Mom would argue the point on Grandma's fashion taste. "And how do you figure this works? Matchmaking is matchmaking, whichever way you look at it."

"Your mother has a thing for matchmaking her daughters with doctors. The doctors she likes wear dull suits, have dull personalities, and drive dull cars."

Hannah turned away and headed indoors, hiding her quiet laughter. She refused to give Grandma any encouragement to matchmake. Hannah didn't need any more boring doctors asking her out on dates, either.

Grandma followed her inside. Hannah rinsed her mug and lid in the kitchen sink. The clubhouse was a large open space with tables and chairs scattered around the room. The changing rooms and restroom facilities were located at the back, beside her office.

A side entry door near the lockers and changing rooms should, in theory, minimize the dirt traipsed through the clubhouse. The teens had their breakfast, took turns using the shower facilities, and left footprints everywhere they walked. It was a routine Hannah knew well from her own junior rowing days.

Hannah had cleared the sink, emptied the dishwasher, packed a second load, and swept the wooden floors before her coffee break. Now the floorboards needed a good wash to mop up the remaining dirt.

"So what do you think?" Grandma asked. "A stuffy doctor with a boring European car, or a good-looking Aussie tiler?"

"There's nothing wrong with European cars." Or distracting Grandma from her original question. Dad's golf sponsors had gifted him at least a dozen cars over the years. The perks from being a golfing pro with a long career in the sporting world.

"European cars have no muscle, not like American cars. The Aussie tiler has a nice smile, an American truck to match his muscles, and a swoony accent to boot."

"Grandma! You need to stop gossiping—"

"It's not gossip if it's true. My friend Rhonda got a quote from him the other day, and she gave me her informed opinion."

Hannah shook her head. "You're impossible, and I'm trying to run a business. I need this tiling job done before spring break, and he's my best option." Her only option in town with openings in March. She couldn't afford this opportunity to be derailed by Grandma scaring him off the premises.

"I could hang around and meet him—"

"Or I could put you to work now cleaning toilets ..."

Grandma raised her brows in mock horror, her cheeky smile firmly in place. "You wouldn't dare. If you want me to continue bringing you coffee ..."

Hannah held her ground. "If you're going to chat and delay my cleaning work, I'll find a spare set of cleaning gloves."

"Oh Hannah, you need to calm down. We could take a selfie

in our cleaning getup. I'm wearing my cute white sneakers, and I'd love to see the look on your mother's face."

Provoking Mom, however tempting, was never a good idea. "I'm going to collect my cleaning stuff now, and the offer to join me still stands."

She walked over to her office and tossed her jacket on the back of her chair. She retrieved a mop, bucket, and two pairs of brand-new cleaning gloves from the storeroom behind the kitchen area.

Hannah placed the gloves on the table closest to Grandma and rolled up the long sleeves of her navy t-shirt. "Are you ready to work, or not? Time is running away from me, and the restrooms need cleaning."

Grandma grinned and walked around the table. She stood on tiptoe and kissed Hannah's cheek. "On second thoughts, my dear, I best be going. I've got a few things to pick up from the store before lunch."

Hannah relaxed her mouth into a smile. The restroom cleaning bluff worked a treat. "Thanks again for the coffee and chat."

"Pleasure. I'll love you and leave you." Grandma collected her purse and headed outdoors.

Peace at last. Hannah converted her ponytail into a messy bun and opened a packet of gloves. She should have the wet areas done in forty minutes tops. Her old denim jeans and comfortable leather hiking boots collected more mud splatters as she took care of the tiled walls and floors.

She finished the wet areas in thirty-five minutes, then refilled the bucket with hot water for the third time. Only the clubhouse wooden floors to go before she could call it a day.

Hannah lifted all the chairs off the floor and arranged them, seats down, on the tabletops. The teens had done a good job wiping down the chairs and tables before they left for school.

With less obstacles to navigate, Hannah whizzed through the mopping.

She finished mopping at the front door opening onto the veranda, using her elbow to wipe perspiration from her brows. Cleaning the clubhouse was a full-on cardio workout. She could skip the gym tonight—guilt free.

Hannah left the bucket full of dirty water and mop on the veranda by the door, tugged off the gloves, and dropped them on the closest bench seat. She lathered her hands with sanitizer from the dispenser inside the door and lowered her weary body onto the bench.

She shut her eyes, her back relaxing against the wooden planks, and focused on her breathing, in and out. A few minutes of rest and recovery before she tackled the next job.

Footsteps crunched on the gravel path leading to the veranda.

"Hey, I'm sorry to disturb you." The strong male voice with a distinctly Australian accent pulled her from a restful state.

Hannah cracked one eye open and jolted awake. She lifted her jaw, closing her mouth into a smile and regaining her composure. Grandma's gossip didn't do the man justice. "Hi." Her voice croaked, sounding like she'd swallowed a pound of dirt.

His smile held her captive, his cornflower blue eyes mirroring her warm welcome. She sat taller in her seat.

"I'm sorry to bother you." He rubbed the back of his neck, his arm muscles strong and flexed under his t-shirt sleeve. "I'm looking for your boss."

His swoony accent was as sweet as a solo guitarist serenading a stranger in a crowd. She could listen to his voice all day long. Hang on. "My boss?"

"Yeah." He checked his phone. "Hannah Gilbertson. She requested a quote for some tiling. Do you know where I can find her?"

She nodded, his words sinking in. He'd mistaken her for the cleaning lady. He must be new to town if he didn't know the boss did everything around here, including the menial tasks.

"Don't let me interrupt your break." His gaze swept over her gloves and nearby mop and bucket, his smile intact. "If you can point me in the right direction."

If he wasn't cute and from Australia, she might take offense at being mistaken for the janitor. She liked him more than she cared to admit.

She stood and held out her hand. "I'm Hannah. Nice to meet you."

His eyes widened and his face darkened to a cute shade of crimson. He shook her hand, his gaze steady.

She could drown in the depths of his eyes, the intensity of their instant connection strong and unexpected. He seemed familiar, with sun-streaked wavy brown hair cropped short at the back and sides, and a tanned complexion from being outdoors, but she couldn't place him.

He let go of her hand. "I'm Joel, and I apologize. I didn't mean to offend you—"

"No." Hannah burst out laughing, appreciating his sincerity. "I'm fine. Have we met before?"

"I don't think so." His expressive blue eyes had shared her mirth, and his posture relaxed. "I'm new to town."

"Okay." Maybe she'd come across Joel's doppelganger. Recognizing faces and voices was a skill she'd practiced for her line of work.

"What tiling work do you need done?"

"Follow me." Her morning had just gotten a whole lot more interesting.

JOEL MANNING FOLLOWED Hannah around the side of the rowing clubhouse toward a back entrance. He was glad he wouldn't be making a mess by walking on any floorboards. The wooden clubhouse had character, and no doubt had a fascinating history. His fascination with its owner, who didn't seem to care that her faded jeans were dotted with dirt, had taken him by surprise.

Talk about how to make a terrible first impression. Seeing Hannah resting on the bench seat after cleaning the floors had led him to draw all the wrong conclusions.

She was sweet to laugh off his mistake and had been professional in her gentle correction.

Hannah stopped at a side door and rubbed the soles of her boots on the door mat. "Don't worry about taking off your work boots."

"Are you sure?" he asked. "I don't mind either way."

"It's all good. The teens were training this morning, and I had to clean to show you the problem areas."

"Okay. Was it the rowing team or the kayaking team?"

"Rowing. The kayakers will train tomorrow morning. Please wait here, and I'll get my notes from my office."

"Sure." He scanned the interior of the clubhouse. Memorabilia hung on the walls along with a large whiteboard schedule. Seven a.m. training starts reminded him of his high school rowing schedule on Sydney Harbour. He didn't miss those cold winter mornings.

Hannah returned holding a tablet. "I took photos of the problem areas." She handed him the tablet and he flicked through the images.

"Do the tiled floors need the grouting fixed, or just the showers?"

"There are broken and chipped floor tiles to replace. I checked with the previous manager, and it's been at least a decade since the floors were refreshed. I'd prefer to use the same color and style as the existing tiles if that's possible."

"Sure." He followed Hannah as she walked through the wet areas and showed him the areas of concern.

"The shower tiling was resealed years ago. They're heavily used, especially in summer. I'm concerned there's water damage in the walls and floors."

"Have you noticed any mold issues?"

"Not that I can see. My maintenance lady does a good job and complies with all the regulations."

"So you're not usually the cleaner?" He couldn't resist teasing her.

She chuckled. "She works at sunset, when it's quiet. I take care of any cleaning during the day."

"You do all the work yourself."

She shook her head. "I usually take Thursday off, and Wednesday or Friday. I start early, by seven. The rest of my team covers the afternoons and my days off. Weekends are our busiest time."

"Those days off are important." A reason why he'd never aspired to have his own business. He liked his weekends, as well as the freedom to work a set roster with a regular salary and less paperwork.

"The previous manager's a lifetime club member who's semi-retired, and he covers my days off."

"That's handy."

"It is. My team are good workers. For the quote, I'd like to repair the floors and reseal the showers to prevent future problems."

He nodded. "A good plan. I'll take a closer look now and write up a quote.

"Thank you, Joel. I appreciate you taking the time to do the quote."

"No worries, and thank you for cleaning up the area. Mud

can hide a lot of problems."

"It was no trouble."

Her smile warmed his heart and piqued his curiosity. He'd almost forgotten she was a potential client when she'd opened her stunning eyes, the color of a clear summer sky, and held his gaze for a long moment. She was right. There was something familiar about Hannah, but he couldn't pin it down.

"I'll need the job done in stages," Hannah said. "The members need access to the restrooms."

"I can accommodate that. Which days are your lightest?"

"Early in the week is quieter."

"Okay. I'll get on with the quote and we can look at dates."

"Sounds good." She pointed to a half-open door. "I'll be in my office if you need me."

He nodded and admired her athletic physique as she walked through to her office. Hannah was an intriguing woman, one he'd like to get to know better. She was confident and smart, and they shared similar interests.

Joel made quick work of assessing the job and putting together a quote plus a potential work schedule. Monday to Wednesday for two weeks should get the job done and still allow the club members reasonable access to the facilities.

He knocked on Hannah's office door, and she signaled for him to enter. He stood in the doorway, waiting for her to end her phone call.

Her messy bun was gone, replaced by a caramel and brown toned ponytail that skimmed the top of her shoulders.

"How'd you go?" she asked.

"All good, and it's a straightforward job. The tiles we'll need to purchase are a common size and color, and available at Cohen's. We won't need to wait on a hardware order."

"That's good news."

He quoted an estimated price and proposed dates when he

had availability in his schedule. "I'll email the details and we can go from there."

Hannah stood. "Thanks again, Joel. I'll get back to you this afternoon when I've looked over the quote and checked the dates will work."

"Okay." He shook her hand, liking her firm grip and soft fingertips. His awareness of her skyrocketed. "Nice doing business with you, Hannah. Is there a good coffee place nearby? I haven't visited this part of town before."

Hannah glanced at her sports watch. "My sister Becky has a coffee cart across the road, near the cabins in the camping ground. We call it RV central, and you can't miss it."

"I know where to look."

"Good. Becky makes the best coffee in town, but I'm biased, and she closes at twelve-thirty. The Bellbird Café in town is your next best coffee option."

"I know the Bellbird. The Aussies I met when I first arrived told me to go there."

"When did you arrive?"

"A few weeks ago. I hit the ground running with work, and I like what I've seen of Trinity Lakes."

"It's a nice town with plenty to do if you like the outdoors."

"That works for me." Now he'd seen this beautiful part of Lake Wainscott, he was itching to get out on the water in a kayak and explore the area. "I'll go find your sister's coffee cart. Would you like me to bring you back something?"

"I'm good, but thanks for the offer. My grandma visits each morning and collects my coffee from Becky."

"Lucky you. I'll send the email soon and look out for your reply this afternoon. Enjoy your day." Joel left the rowing club and cut across the gravel parking lot toward the road.

A long and flat cycling path hugged the lake for at least a mile leading into the main part of town where the lake narrowed into a river. His maps app showed that the cycling path heading in the other direction, away from town, left the lake and joined a back road heading to the highway and the mountains.

A fit couple with a jogging pram ran along the path toward town. Two older kids sat on the end of a dock, dangling fishing lines in the water. A lone man, wearing a shabby version of what Joel now recognized as the city employee work uniform, carried a bulky trash bag and bent to pick up something from the ground.

The parkland along the pristine foreshores benefited from the man's diligence and commitment to his job.

When the weather warmed up, Joel hoped to cycle from town along the lake and climb the scenic mountain road. He wasn't into skiing, but he'd heard the mountain resort was popular with tourists.

He crossed the road and walked over to a red coffee cart with a candy-striped awning and a few small tables shaded by matching umbrellas. He nodded to the family eating pastries at one of the tables and moved to the head of the line.

Becky gave him a big smile, her resemblance to her sister striking. "Hey Joel, it's good to meet you. Hannah said you were heading over. What would you like?"

Joel acknowledged her greeting and scanned her chalkboard drinks menu. "A cappuccino with whole milk, no sugar, please."

"Coming right up. Regular or large?"

"Regular is fine, thanks." The familiar freshly ground coffee bean aroma lingered in the breeze. He ignored the tempting pastries in the display case, knowing they'd be loaded with sugar, and read the food menu. "You sell real meat pies?"

"We sure do." Becky's attention stayed on the coffee machine beside the bakery case. "The bakery who supplies my pastries has always made the Aussie style beef meat pies. They're very popular and taste good with ketchup."

Yes, tomato sauce was what they called ketchup back home.

He'd already made that blunder and confused a server. "I usually buy a pie at the footy."

"The footy?" Becky tipped her head to the side, her eyes on the milk frothing in a stainless-steel jug. "I'm not sure I know what you mean."

"Sorry—football. What we call Rugby Union or Rugby League or AFL, depending on where we are in Australia. Not soccer."

"Oh, I know what AFL is. It's fun to watch all the kicking around the field."

"Really? Do they play AFL here in Trinity Lakes?" He was staying at the Bible college accommodation in town with the international students, but he hadn't heard about an AFL competition.

"Once a year, in April, there's an AFL game played for fun in town. If you play AFL, you should sign up."

Joel grinned. "I'm more of a rugby guy, but I can play AFL. I'll ask around."

"The guys at the Bible college where you're staying can tell you all about it."

He paused, drawing his eyebrows together. "You know where I'm living?"

Becky snickered. "Trinity Lakes is a small town, and everyone knows everyone else's business. News travels fast around here." She placed his cappuccino on the counter.

"Okay." He pulled out his wallet.

"No, your coffee is already paid for."

"Free coffee. How do you stay in business?"

"It's on Hannah's tab. She's keen to secure your services and seal the deal."

He smiled. "Thank you, and please pass on my thanks to Hannah." He'd book Hannah's job in his schedule when his boss approved his quote and Hannah paid the holding deposit.

"Will do." Becky handed him a card. "I take same-day orders online, if you're wanting a meat pie. I sometimes sell out early."

"Thanks." He sipped his cappuccino, appreciating the rich flavor. Hannah wasn't wrong about the quality. "This is good, and I'll be back. Are you open every day?"

"I'm here most mornings. I'm usually set up by eight at the latest, and I update my trading hours online. If the weather forecast is wet and windy and horrible, it's not worth my time setting up the cart."

"That makes sense. I heard it snows here during winter."

She nodded. "Snow days are a thing, and I don't open. The advantage of having a portable business I can tow anywhere."

"It definitely reduces overheads and provides flexibility."

Becky nodded again, her gaze shifting to look at something over his shoulder.

Another customer arrived and Joel moved, taking a seat at an empty table. The lake was visible across the road, and a small sailing club was situated on the other side of the parking lot, closer to town. An old boat shed was further along, and the rest of the shore that he could see toward town was beautiful with green open spaces.

He sipped his cappuccino, appreciating the blessing of landing a flexible and well-paid job with affordable accommodation in Trinity Lakes. The pace of life was much slower than Sydney, and he'd secured a twelve-month work visa that gave him the freedom to explore the rest of the country in the coming months.

His attraction to Hannah was unexpected, and she hadn't been wearing wedding rings. Not that he should be noticing such details. It didn't matter if Hannah was single or in a relationship. Joel had prayed about this trip, and starting over in a new place where everyone at church and in his social circle didn't know the woman he'd loved and wanted to marry had dumped him.

His ex had her reasons, and it wasn't his place to share her personal information and correct the wrong assumptions made by people who'd blamed him for their failed relationship. A year away from home, with no romantic entanglements to cause him grief, was the medicine he needed to cure his wounded heart.

He looked forward to working in Hannah's rowing club and hoped they could become friends. They lived on opposite sides of the globe, and a lasting relationship that was deeper than friendship wasn't an option.

CHAPTER TWO

Two weeks later, Hannah sat in her office on Monday morning and blew out a frustrated breath. The cash and coins were bundled and bagged inside the petty cash box on her desk. She'd counted them three times, but the paper receipt totals from the weekend weren't matching the corresponding equipment hire records.

The teens who worked with her on the weekend were usually accurate with their money handling. The electronic records of card and online payments were balanced. She must have missed a coupon or a discounted rate somewhere in the pile of receipts that would explain the small cash discrepancy.

Hannah rolled her shoulders and stretched out her arms and legs. Sunlight filtered in through her office window, the lake gleaming in front of the beautiful blue sky mountain backdrop.

If only she could be out on the water. Instead, she'd been sitting at her desk all morning, counting money, balancing the books, and catching up on email and other administrative tasks. The weekend tourist trade had been busier than anticipated, which was good, and she was ready for Grandma to return with two coffees—a latte for her and a cappuccino for Joel.

She could hear Joel working and moving around, occasionally chipping away at something. The tiles he'd purchased from Cohen's were a perfect match, and he'd warned her that it could be a noisy morning indoors.

Grandma peeked her head into Hannah's office. "Break time."

"Yay. I'll be there in a few minutes."

"I already told Joel his coffee is here."

"Thanks." Hannah locked away the receipts with the petty cash box to deal with later. A run into town and a visit to the bank could wait until her shift changeover with her friend, Tabby, this afternoon. Tabby worked at her family's B&B inn up the road in the mornings.

Hannah walked outside onto the veranda and found Grandma in an animated conversation with Joel. He wore an old t-shirt and cargo pants, and looked like he couldn't feel the early spring chill in the air. His tanned forearms displayed strong muscles that reminded her of a rower or kayaker's build. He probably spent time in the gym using weights and rowing machines.

Grandma's smile and voice held a mischievous air. "Hannah, my dear, here's your latte."

"Thanks, Grandma." She sat beside Grandma, and diagonally opposite Joel who'd brought a chair outside with a wide armrest for his cup.

"I hope the noise isn't bothering you." Joel picked up his coffee mug. "Gracie said she could hear me from the parking lot."

"It's fine." So Joel was already on a first name basis with Grandma. How long had they been talking? "I've got work to do in the boat shed next." She needed to check the inventory of kayaks, canoes, and other equipment, and ensure they were in good condition and met safety standards. They'd only lost one oar to the bottom of the lake over the weekend.

"That's good timing for Joel." Grandma said. "I have a crochet class this morning."

Joel nodded. "I've heard about the emporium in town. People travel for miles to do classes."

"They sure do." Grandma turned to Joel. "Hannah would rather read books for her book club than do crafts."

Joel's gaze switched to Hannah. "Book clubs can be fun. What do you like reading?"

"Mainly fiction. We choose a different genre each month."

Grandma fluttered her eyelashes. "Romance is her all-time favorite, Joel."

He grinned. "Is that so?"

Hannah lowered her gaze and sipped her latte. Grandma's class couldn't start soon enough. "I mostly read Christian fiction. And the classics, of course."

"I've already told Joel you were smart and did a business degree instead of majoring in English lit," Grandma said.

Hannah narrowed her eyes. "Grandma, what else have you been telling Joel?"

"Oh, just this and that. Nothing important." Grandma stood. "Class is starting soon, and I'll see you both tomorrow for coffee."

Hannah and Joel said goodbye to Grandma, and then Hannah took the bait thrown by Grandma.

"What exactly did my grandma say?"

"A lot." His eyes sparkled. "Let's see if I can remember it right."

Oh boy. "Please tell me she didn't tell you my entire life story."

He laughed. "Only the highlights."

"I hope they're good."

"I think so. You grew up here, and Gracie is proud of your college achievements. She loves that you moved back home near her. You're an awesome rowing and kayaking instructor, and your summer kayaking tour groups are fun."

"Wow. She was chatty." Grandma had ignored all her requests and blabbed her entire bio. Sigh.

"There's more," he said.

Ugh. Of course there was more. "What else did she say?"

"She talked about your family, and how she lives with your mother. Your dad and older brother are pro golfers. Your baby sister has a college tennis scholarship in Florida, where your dad and brother live. And, years ago, your father was mayor of Trinity Lakes."

"Now you know my life story and family history. We're big on sports, except for Becky and Mom."

He sipped his cappuccino. "Becky makes amazing coffee that beats all the sporting achievements."

She chuckled. "I won't argue that point. Leanna—she's in Florida—and I are good at sports, but we don't have the drive our brother, Dan, has to make it a professional career like Dad."

"I can imagine the pro golfing lifestyle and all the travel is exciting and also hard work."

"Dad and Dan are driven to succeed. I prefer coaching to competing. It's rewarding to watch the younger kids, especially, succeed and achieve their goals."

"Is this where you trained and learned how to row?"

She nodded. "I've turned down career opportunities in New York and other cities to do what I love here. Best decision ever. Speaking of work, I'd better get back to it."

Joel finished his cappuccino and stood. "Thanks again for the coffee."

"You're welcome. Grandma is always reliable for coffee." And always reliable for embarrassing her again tomorrow.

Joel carried his coffee mug and chair indoors, then returned to his tiling work. Hannah collected her tablet and headed out the side door to the boat shed next to the parking lot. She buzzed open one of the roller garage doors facing the lake and methodically worked her way around the shed, taking notes on what needed to be ordered and replaced.

Her stomach grumbled, reminding her that she needed to break for lunch. Her friend Leah from the organic foods store had stopped by at seven-thirty, before Joel arrived, and delivered Hannah's weekly fruit breakfast order for the high school students.

Leah had included a healthy spinach salad for Hannah's lunch in the order, a nice and welcome treat.

Hannah closed the boat shed roller door and made her way to the kitchen. Joel had handwashed both mugs and lids and left them to air dry on the dish drainer. Did the man have any faults?

She took her salad out of the fridge and put it beside a napkin and fork on the countertop. Footsteps sounded near the door. Many of the senior members were around the clubhouse today, taking advantage of the dry weather and a wisp of a breeze on the lake. They often had lunch at the picnic tables near the dock.

"Hannah, you're here! I was hoping to see you."

Her stomach forgot it was hungry and sank faster than a stone tossed into the lake. What was Richie doing here? She turned around and forced her reluctant mouth into a polite smile. "I'm here, like always. Why have you stopped by?"

He stepped toward her and gave her an awkward hug. "I'm here to visit you, of course. Dan mentioned you were doing some renovations."

She took a few steps to the side, putting space between them, and furrowed her brows. It was at least a week, maybe two weeks, since she'd been in contact with her brother. Had she talked about the tiling with Dan?

"I'm tiling the wet areas. No big deal." She could see Joel's boots through the open changing room door. She hoped he had his earbuds in like earlier when he'd been lifting the old tiles.

"I missed seeing you at church last night. Was everything okay?"

"I worked late and watched the livestream at home." Surprisingly, her mother hadn't told her Richie was in town. In recent months Mom never missed an opportunity to push Hannah into dating her brother's best friend from high school, who was now a doctor based in Spokane.

"I visited with your mom this morning, and she suggested I stop by and see you. Have you had lunch?"

"Not yet." What was Mom scheming this time? Hannah pointed to the salad container on the countertop. "I'll eat and work in my office." A plan she'd hatched within seconds of hearing him mention Mom.

He looked around. "It's quiet today. You should have thirty minutes to spare for a dedicated lunch break."

If friendship was all Richie wanted, she'd give him hours of her time. She missed the easy relationship they used to enjoy before her mother started meddling. "I'm sorry, Richie. Lunch isn't going to happen." Not today, and not any other day after he'd spent time with Mom. Why couldn't he take the hint and listen to her instead of Mom?

"How about dinner tomorrow night? I'm only in town for a week, and I'm working at the clinic until late today."

"Sorry, I can't." She looked outside and spotted the Junk Man hovering near the gravel path. Like clockwork, he stopped by each day for his morning break.

"Richie, I have things to do. Please excuse me." She moved to the kitchen counter and switched on the electric kettle.

"You don't need to make me coffee." Richie leaned back against the counter, looking like he could stay for the afternoon.

"I'm not. But you can help yourself. Make a hot drink or

have a cookie." Seriously, why would he think her world revolved around him and his needs?

Hannah filled a thermos with spoonfuls of instant coffee and sugar, stirring in hot water from the kettle. She used a napkin to pluck a chocolate chip cookie out of the jar, picked up the thermos, and walked out to the veranda.

The Junk Man kept his distance, like usual, and nodded to acknowledge the food and drink. Hannah walked along the gravel path and placed the thermos and napkin-wrapped cookie on a picnic table that sat on its own, away from the cycle path and the seniors who were lunching together at the club. She smiled and waved at the seniors before heading indoors.

Richie stood inside the doorway, his arms folded across his chest. "Are you now feeding homeless people with club resources?"

"Richie!" Her voice ratcheted up another few decibels. She walked past him, anger driving every step toward the kitchen area.

He followed her. "Can we talk about this situation?"

She turned to face him, hands on hips. "What situation? Stop being a snob. He's not homeless, and how I run my club is not your concern."

Joel's boots were still visible in the changing room. If Joel wasn't wearing earbuds, he'd hear every word of her loud conversation with Richie.

Richie took a step closer. "People like him aren't good for business. The hobos and their unusual habits discourage the tourist trade."

She stepped back. "I don't need a lecture, and you don't know anything about him."

"That's not true. I see his type when I work in the ER. People like him can be mentally unstable and dangerous. I'm concerned for your safety."

Oh, please. Now it was about her safety. "Have you noticed

the foreshores along the lake, including my land, are tidy with no trash?"

He shrugged. "I guess so. It's not something I look for, to be honest."

"He works for the city and takes care of this part of the lake. He cleans up the trash that's left and washes up on my land, for free. The least I can do is give him coffee and cookies."

"Please tell me he's not the hermit with geese. One of my patients has complained numerous times about the stress and anxiety caused by a neighbor who works for the city and fits his description."

Hannah let out an exasperated sigh. "I don't know about any geese, and I'm not interested in town gossip."

"It's not gossip, Hannah. I'm a doctor, and I know the warning signs. Please listen to me. Your safety is important."

"I'll be fine, and I've got work to do. Please excuse me." She collected her salad, walked into her office, and closed the door behind her.

When would Mom stop meddling? Richie was misguided, but he wasn't a bad guy. They'd grown up together and had been friends for years. He was a few years older than her, and he'd been part of the rowing team who'd traveled out of town for meets.

Hannah had admired how hard Richie had worked to obtain his rowing scholarship and medical degree in Seattle. His success had spurred her on to chase a college scholarship.

Had Joel overheard her conversation with Richie? Talk about piling embarrassment on top of embarrassment. Between Grandma's good intentions and Mom's pushy interfering, she'd be shocked if Joel wanted to be friends with her.

Joel was a great guy, although it was unlikely he'd still be in Trinity Lakes by this time next year. Typical that the one guy who had caught her eye was only passing through town. Joel was destined to return to Australia and his home on the other side of the world.

———

JOEL WASHED his hands in the rowing club restroom, ready to break for lunch, head outdoors, and collect the meat pie he'd ordered from Becky. He'd made good progress this morning and hoped to finish up early today.

He grabbed his backpack and walked into the main area of the clubhouse. A guy, presumably Richie, sat at a table on his own. An uneaten cookie was on a plate beside his coffee mug.

Ten minutes earlier, Joel had heard Hannah's office door close with a loud thud. Joel hadn't wanted to eavesdrop, but the frustration in Hannah's voice, paired with Richie's arrogant tone, had carried their entire conversation into his work area.

Joel nodded at Richie. "Have you seen Hannah?"

"She's in her office, and I don't think she wants to be disturbed." Richie stared at Hannah's closed door, ignoring Joel's presence.

"No worries." He left the clubhouse, happy to be away from the well-dressed doctor in a dark mood. Joel sent Hannah a quick message, letting her know he was taking an hour for lunch.

He decided to stretch his legs and loop along the foreshore before collecting his pie. He left the rowing club and strode toward town on the wide cycling path. The breeze off the lake cooled his face, and he appreciated the fresh outdoor air. He walked by the parking lot between the rowing and sailing clubs, and further along toward a dilapidated old boat shed.

A few sailing dinghies and a number of kayakers were taking advantage of the nice weather on the lake. Club members had ducked in and out of the rowing club at different times during the morning. They were mostly seniors, and they'd thanked him for the work he was doing for their club.

The open spaces around the lake reminded him of Australia, and the coastal lagoon near where he lived on Sydney's northern beaches. He'd learned a lot about Hannah from her sweet grandma, who was a load of fun.

He rounded the old boat shed and cut across the road where a cute B&B inn had uninterrupted lakefront views. Why would the doctor hang around when Hannah had made it clear she was busy?

Joel's lunch break disappeared too fast, and he went back indoors and back to work. The doctor was gone, and Hannah was unloading the dishwasher.

"Hey Joel, how's the tiling going?"

"Pretty good. I'm making progress on the showers."

"Can I take a look?"

"Sure. Watch your step on the floor." He showed her the work he'd already done, and his plans for the afternoon.

She peeked into a shower stall. "Will you need the full six days?"

"I think so. I'll be here each morning at seven, but I may finish early—around lunchtime or a bit later. I'll work on the floor tiles in each area last."

"Okay. Please let me know if you need anything."

"I'll try to be quiet and not bother you."

She leaned against the changing room doorframe, her mouth slanting into a small frown. "Um, I'm sorry about the commotion earlier."

"It's none of my business, Hannah."

"But it's my fault if Richie was unpleasant. He mentioned he saw you before you went to lunch."

"He was fine." Joel shrugged. "No big deal."

"Except you heard our conversation."

He nodded. "I think it's good you take care of the worker."

Unlike Richie, Joel could acknowledge that the man was diligent and deserving of Hannah's hospitality.

"He's known as the Junk Man, and some people share Richie's attitude."

Not surprising. He held Hannah's defiant gaze, choosing his words before opening his mouth. "I do agree with Richie that your safety is important."

"But the Junk Man's not making me feel unsafe."

"From what I've seen, you spend a lot of time working here on your own."

She crossed her arms over her torso, not giving an inch. "I promise you, he's never threatened me or Becky. He sits at the same table each day and leaves the empty thermos on the veranda."

"That's considerate of him." The Junk Man didn't sound like he'd cause Hannah any problems.

She nodded, her eyes softening and arms dropping to her sides. "The previous manager, who still works here, gave him a coffee thermos and cookies for years before I took over."

"I bet the Junk Man has a story." Joel could only imagine how the man had ended up living a hermit-like existence.

"I'm sure he does. I'll repay kindness with kindness, and not be bullied by Richie—or anyone else—into treating him differently."

"That's fair. Walking the love your neighbor talk is important but isn't easy."

Hannah lifted a brow. "Are you studying at the Bible college?"

He shook his head. "My father knew people at the college, and that's how I landed in Trinity Lakes."

"From a church connection with the college."

He nodded. "Like you, my parents split up years ago. Mum remarried, we stayed in Sydney, and I have a half-sister and brother. They're much younger than me. Then Dad remarried and moved to Adelaide, and that's where he met people connected to Trinity Lakes and the summer camp."

"Oh, you're also doing summer camp? I used to volunteer during my summer college vacations. It's so much fun."

"That's my plan. I've discovered the camp is out of town and located on a different lake."

She smiled. "Three lakes and three old bridges—hence the town name."

"Interesting. I've only seen two lakes and two bridges."

"Lake Wainscott is by far the biggest. The stone bridge over the lake in the center of town, where it narrows into a river flowing west, is the prettiest bridge. You probably haven't seen the third bridge—it's on this road, heading further out of town into the mountains."

"Ah, that explains it. I know of a bridge on the outskirts of town leading to the mountain highway."

She nodded. "That southern bridge spans the narrow section of a different river that joins the second and third lakes. Although, the third lake is tiny. It's really just a large pond in a golf course."

"Can you kayak between all the lakes?"

"In theory, yes. There's a river system that joins the three lakes. We operate tour groups during summer."

"That sounds fun."

"It is, although there's a section of the river in the mountain foothills to our east that we call the rapids. It can be tricky to navigate at different times during summer. When the river's swollen, it's dangerous, even for experienced kayakers."

"It sounds like something I'd like to explore."

"Do you row or kayak?"

"Both. I live on the coast in Sydney near a lagoon. A fun way to exercise."

"The best." Hannah's smile widened. "I'm going to take my kayak out this afternoon, sometime between three-thirty and four. You're welcome to join me if you like. I have all the equipment you'll need. A perk of the job."

"Sounds great. I'll be finishing here around two and can be back by three-thirty."

"We have a deal. Catch you later." She disappeared into her office.

Joel topped up his water bottle and returned to the changing room, storing his backpack in a corner near his tools. Hannah's invitation to kayak this afternoon was a great first step in becoming friends outside of a work context. He wasn't interested in a relationship, and nor was she—listening to her rebuff the doctor reinforced that.

He knew all about rejection. Eighteen months earlier, his ex-girlfriend from church had dumped him and taken off on a mission trip to Europe. The sting of rejection had lessened over time. Her explanation for why she'd dumped him, which she'd shared six months after their split, had given him closure. The failed relationship had inspired him to move outside his comfort zone and temporarily relocate to Trinity Lakes. He looked forward to kayaking with Hannah after work.

CHAPTER THREE

Ten days later, Hannah turned over fresh salmon filets in her frying pan. Tonight was book club, and she loved having an early dinner at home with friends before they drove into town to the Bellbird Café.

Whole potatoes wrapped in aluminum foil baked in her oven. Sliced vegetables were steaming on the stove, and the condiments for their potatoes were ready to serve on the kitchen island.

Tabby laid out three place settings on the table adjacent to the island, which overlooked the deck. Leah was on her way from the organics store with Hannah's grocery order. Becky's ginger calico cat, Mischief, sat perched on a bar stool at the island, eyeing the sour cream.

Hannah gave Mischief the stink eye. "Don't you dare go near the cream."

Tabby laughed and flicked straight blonde hair back over her shoulders. "As if Mischief will ever listen to you. She won't even do what Becky asks."

"True." Hannah placed their dinner plates beside the condiments and relocated the cream further away from Mischief. "That sounds like Leah."

Leah breezed into the kitchen, carrying two full recycled cloth grocery bags. "Sorry I'm late. I was held up by a customer who walked in two minutes before closing."

"You're right on time." Hannah turned off the heat and moved the salmon to a serving plate. "Thanks for bringing the groceries."

"No problem." Leah grinned, showing gleaming white teeth. She didn't drink tea or coffee, so probably didn't need artificial whitening. The girl wouldn't dare use chemicals in her mouth.

Tabby helped Leah unpack the groceries and store the items in Hannah's pantry and fridge.

"Thanks, girls. I appreciate your help."

"It's no trouble," Tabby said. "Your kitchen is our second home."

Hannah chuckled. Her friends were familiar with her spacious kitchen, and they occasionally cooked here as well.

"Is Becky having dinner with us?" Leah tucked a loose strand of blonde hair behind her ear.

"Not tonight." Hannah retrieved the potatoes from the oven and added them to the collection of food on the kitchen island. "She has something going on in town. She'll meet us at the Bellbird."

"Becky loves Carla Laureano's books, and I didn't think she'd want to miss out on book club tonight," Tabby said.

"I really liked reading Provenance, and I read it fast." Leah gave a fake swoon, resting her hand to her forehead.

"Me, too." Hannah giggled and passed a plate to Leah. "It was that good, I couldn't put it down. I hid in my office, door closed, and finished the last five chapters when I should have been invoicing."

Tabby chuckled. "So that's why you left the invoicing for me. Thanks." Irony dripped from her words.

Leah cut open her potato and piled on the toppings. "The accounting for my little shop is time consuming, too."

"But it keeps the cash flowing in." Hannah added salmon to her plate and layered steamed asparagus on top of her potato. Mischief had heeded her warning and cleared out, leaving the sour cream untouched. She added grated cheese and took a seat at the table.

"Speaking of cash flow." Tabby scooted her chair closer to the table. "Dad says it's time for me to renovate Gran's rooms and expand the Inn."

Hannah nodded. "That'll take a lot of time, or money, or both."

"Dad says we have some money, but I don't know if I'm ready to clear out Gran's rooms yet. The memories ..."

Leah sipped her water. "What about the old boat shed? Your family owns that land, right?"

"No, the Inn's land stops at the road. I don't know who owns the boat shed. I think Dad said it's owned by some kind of trust, and there's something weird about the zoning."

"It would be great if someone could do something with that land." The mayor had told Hannah they wanted the old boat shed demolished as soon as possible. "There's plenty of tourists looking to do more water sports on weekends. Would you believe all our kayaks were in use on Saturday?"

"It was busy in town over the weekend, and I was run off my feet. The weather was nice for March." Leah leaned back in her chair.

"It was," Tabby said. "Our B&B was fully booked Friday to Sunday as well. Another reason to renovate and expand."

"And spring break is still weeks away." Hannah sliced up her salmon tail, checked for bones, and added a spoonful of dill mayonnaise.

Tabby swirled the water in her glass, her brows drawn

together. "Hannah, do you know anything about the zoning of the lakefront land?"

"Not really. Dad said we can't renovate and expand the rowing club or the sailing club building because it's in a flood zone."

"Interesting." Leah nibbled her bottom lip. "I didn't know that part of the lake flooded."

Hannah nodded. "I haven't seen or heard about flooding, either. By memory, Dad said it could be a one in a hundred years flood event—or maybe one in five hundred years. The zoning change happened twenty-something years ago, around the time he purchased the land."

"When your dad was mayor?" Tabby asked.

"Maybe. I know Dad wanted to be mayor to get the country club and golf course redevelopment across the line, but I don't know if he had ambitions to redevelop the waterfront. It's not something he's mentioned."

"Gran would have known. She knew more local stories than Rhonda Ingalls."

"Yeah, and your gran knew the true stories." If only Rhonda would mind her own business. The notorious gossip, Grandma's friend, thought she knew everything about everyone.

Tabby tapped her chin. "Changing the subject, I ran into Kyla today."

"Your favorite person." Leah's tone dripped with sarcasm. "What happened?"

"I mentioned book club was on tonight. A benign topic you'd think, like the weather."

Hannah nodded. "Who doesn't like book club?"

"Apparently Kyla," Tabby said.

"No, really?" Leah frowned, as if not participating in the book club was an unpardonable sin. "Why does she have a problem with book club?"

"Kyla said she can't attend because she's a youth group leader and has to set a good example for the teens."

"What's going to book club got to do with church and youth group?" Hannah sipped her sparkling water. Kyla was dedicated and did a lot of volunteer work for their church. Hannah worked weekends, and her busy work schedule limited her church involvement.

"I'm confused." Leah shook her head. "We often select Christian fiction books, and we avoid steamy romances and novels with violent content."

"Kyla said, and I quote, 'the book club isn't Christian enough because you read fiction books.' She also said she doesn't have time to waste on stories that aren't true, when she could be studying the Bible."

"Seriously?" Leah scoffed and lifted her palms. "I have no words."

Hannah's mouth gaped. "Maybe she didn't intend to sound rude. Sometimes we say stuff we regret later." Mom would do that and refuse to acknowledge her words were inappropriate. She'd never apologize either.

"I'm sorry, Hannah." Tabby let out a sigh. "I know Kyla is always nice to you, but this is typical of the type of things she says to me."

Hannah shook her head. "I don't understand why she'd want to hurt you. Book club won't be everyone's jam, but there's no need to be mean."

"I can see how Kyla could draw that conclusion." Leah rolled her eyes. "Her whole life revolves around church and church activities. It's her loss."

Tabby nodded. "And our gain. We don't need negative people when we're just trying to encourage reading."

"A good point." Hannah said. "Not everyone at book club is connected to a church, and we want everyone to feel welcome."

"And reading is subjective. We're not all going to like the

same things." Leah stabbed at a piece of salmon. "I feel comfortable sharing my thoughts at the book club and knowing the group will respect what I say. We happily agree to disagree."

Tabby nodded. "Which is what I love. People like Kyla want to take control, and we don't need that group dynamic."

"I agree we don't need troublemakers." Hannah blew out a long breath. Why couldn't people just get along? "I haven't seen that side of Kyla, but Tabby, I do believe what you're saying is true."

Hannah wished Kyla would show Tabby some grace and not always be critical. Walking the talk, as Joel had said, was what Jesus would do. Hannah wasn't perfect and made her share of mistakes, but she tried to be kind to others. Tabby had a big heart, and she didn't need Kyla's insults or mean words. Especially not when she was still raw from the pain of losing her dear gran, who'd raised Tabby and her two siblings.

"So, Hannah." Tabby gave a sly grin. "Have you told Leah about your new rowing partner?"

"Oh, it's good you found someone." Leah tilted her head. "Can she keep up with you on the water?"

Hannah nodded. "It's working out well, and he pushes me to go harder and challenge myself."

Leah's eyes widened. "He? Who's this mystery man? Have I met him?"

"You've met him." Hannah held back a goofy grin that wanted to break free. "Remember Joel, the tiler you met on Monday."

"Hannah, you've been holding out on us. He's cute, and built, and an Aussie. You go, girl." Leah waggled a finger.

Tabby clapped her hands, bouncing in her seat. "That's what I said. He's dreamy and, from what I've seen, I think he's into Hannah."

"No, we're friends. Nothing more." She'd now included Joel, if he was available, in her mid-afternoon rowing and kayaking training schedule. They worked similar hours and Joel enjoyed her water workout routine. He'd signed up as a rowing club member, too.

"Will he go to the gym at the country club?" Leah raised a brow. "I can look out for him when I do my food deliveries there."

"I don't think so. He's made friends at the Bible college campus, and I know he works out and plays sports with them as well."

Tabby gave a wistful smile. "He really is your perfect match. He loves sports, copes with your training regime, and he's a nice guy."

"I don't know about that." Hannah rubbed at her temples. Her friends would be arranging a bridal shower next if she didn't watch her words.

Tabby touched her throat. "Every afternoon this week when I've been working with you at the rowing club, he's turned up on time, ready to row or kayak or do whatever you suggest. The man is smitten."

Leah laughed. "I'm with Tabby on this one. He sounds like a keeper. Why don't you ask him out?"

Hannah pushed out a long breath. If only it was that simple, like a fairytale coming true. Happy endings in real life were never guaranteed. "He was my contractor until he finished the job yesterday. We're friends, and that works for me." It was for the best. If she told herself that enough times, she might start to believe it.

"I assume he goes to church somewhere, if he's staying at the college?" Tabby's eyes sparkled.

"I guess so." Hannah had mentioned to Joel that she attended the Sunday evening service at her church in town. He had Sunday mornings free, and he probably went to a service with his college friends at one of the other churches in Trinity Lakes.

Tabby and Leah had her best interests at heart, but they were wrong about Joel. Hannah acknowledged the attraction and the flip-flopping in her belly at the thought of seeing him. The tingles couldn't be ignored, even though they should be ignored.

Dating Joel was a bad idea. That was the only conclusion that made sense. A romantic relationship with Joel could only lead to heartbreak when he left her behind and moved home to Australia.

———

JOEL ARRIVED EARLY for church on Sunday evening and waited in his truck for Hannah. He didn't know what the parking situation would be like, and it was easier to find a space for his truck on Main Street.

He'd spent the weekend with his new friends from the Bible college. Campus life in the dorms had its perks. There was always something fun happening, or something interesting to volunteer to do. His new friends also shared his love for sports, and he'd been too busy to experience any real loneliness from being in a foreign country away from his family and friends.

He opened his phone to catch up on messages from home. Tiny pangs of homesickness spiked his heart as he read Dad's cheerful message with woeful attempts at emoji humor. He missed Dad and his stepmum, Lisa, who lived in Adelaide, South Australia. Joel enjoyed making the long and scenic inland road trip from Sydney to Adelaide to visit with them.

The next message made him smile. Zach, his friend from church in Sydney, and Zach's wife, Billie, would be visiting Trinity Lakes at the end of March. Joel had sent Zach information on Tabby's family's B&B, and their accommodation booking at the Inn was confirmed. Joel planned to work less during Zach and Billie's midweek visit so he could do fun, touristy things with them.

The last message created worry lines on his forehead. Mum

was having trouble managing Bella, his increasingly rebellious fourteen-year-old sister. It didn't help that his stepdad, Mike, was working in New Zealand, and all the parenting responsibilities had fallen on Mum's shoulders. Joel gave her a sympathetic ear in his response, and prayed the family situation would improve soon.

Joel spotted Hannah's SUV pulling into the church parking lot. He put his phone in his pocket, locked his truck, and walked over to meet her. He'd messaged Hannah earlier in the day, asking if she was attending the service tonight. She'd talked about her church during their frequent rowing and kayaking training sessions over the last few weeks, and had invited him to come along sometime.

Hannah beeped her SUV locked and smiled. "I'm glad you could make it tonight."

He nodded, his smile matching hers. "Your sales pitch worked."

She chuckled. "No church is perfect, but the teaching is solid, and they do a lot of good work in the community helping people in need."

"I'm looking forward to the service." Helping people seemed to be the small-town way, and different to his faster-paced life in Sydney.

Joel fell into step beside her. They walked along the sidewalk and reached the front entrance of the church building. "Is there a place you normally sit?"

Hannah shook her head. "I'm usually arriving right on time or a few minutes late so sit wherever I can find a seat."

The building was filling up as people filed in ahead and behind them and spread out into the rows.

"How about over there." He pointed to a section of seating on the side toward the back. "I've never been a front row kind of guy."

"Me, either." She snickered. "You're not a preacher's kid."

"Nope. My father considered doing ministry work for all of five seconds. But he's still very involved in his local church and supporting various ministries. Just not in a pastoral position."

"It's good that your family are believers."

"Mum stopped going to church years ago, although I know she prays and still has faith. My stepdad is an atheist."

"That's complicated."

"It sure is." He stood back, allowing Hannah to walk ahead and claim a seat.

She settled in her seat and turned toward him, meeting his gaze. "What does your stepdad think of your church involvement, and living on a Bible college campus?"

"I honestly don't know about the campus thing." Joel had seen Mike at Christmas, and he couldn't remember what they'd talked about during their hot summer Christmas Day festivities. Mike had bailed on going to the beach with his children after Christmas lunch. Joel had filled in, and enjoyed playing in the surf with Bella and their younger brother, Jack, while Mum and Mike stayed home and fought about something. Joel couldn't help wondering if the New Zealand job was disguising a marital separation, although Mum had denied it.

Hannah let out a small sigh. "I'm guessing you probably don't talk to him about church-related stuff."

"Not really. Mike is a you-do-you type of person, and money is the most important thing in his life."

"More important than family?"

"Sadly, I think so. He's currently living and working in New Zealand."

Her eyes widened. "Without your mother?"

"Yeah, Bella and Jack are established in private schools in Sydney with their friends, and it would be disruptive to move them overseas for only six months." The excuses sounded reasonable, and he hoped they reflected the truth.

"That makes sense, I guess."

He nodded. Bella's underage drinking with her wild group of friends at sleepovers was becoming a regular thing Mum couldn't seem to stop. An absent father wasn't helping and could be the catalyst for some of his sister's reckless behavior.

The service leader spoke into the microphone, and Joel switched his focus to the front of the church. He was glad he'd accepted Hannah's invitation, and he looked forward to worshiping with her. He liked spending time with Hannah, and he hoped they'd have an opportunity to continue doing more things together.

———

HANNAH STOOD for the closing song, distracted by the man standing close beside her. She'd been hyperaware of the sideways looks from friends and members of the congregation who'd noticed she'd arrived with Joel.

Fatigue from her long day at work and her rush to eat an early dinner before church because she'd skipped a proper lunch break was catching up with her. Soon she'd be hiding yawns and apologizing to Joel for appearing bored.

There was nothing boring about Joel. Their shared passion for her favorite sporting activities had given them plenty of time to talk, and she was intrigued by his description of life in Australia.

The pastor closed out the service, and Hannah turned to Joel. "What's your verdict?"

"I like it, and I'd like to come back."

"I'm glad." The warmth from his smile stretched out to encompass the top of her head and the tips of her toes. "Want to stay for supper?"

He shook his head. "It's almost my bedtime."

"Yeah, I can relate." She stifled a small yawn. "I'd go to a morning service if it didn't clash with work."

"I like morning services. The guys from college go to a few different churches in town, and I tag along."

She nodded. "It sounds convenient."

"It works for me. We often have breakfast together beforehand."

"How fun. Reminds me of living on campus in Boston. Everything was close by, and I didn't need a car."

"Did you like living in Boston?"

"I did." She cherished many good memories from her college years. "It's a lovely city, full of history and a lot to see and do. Are you planning a visit?"

He nodded. "A few of the guys are talking about summer road trip routes. Heading to the east coast via Chicago is one idea."

"The Great Lakes are beautiful, and a must-see if you're driving east."

"Niagara Falls is near the top of my list."

"Definitely go there. Do you have a visa for Canada?"

"Not yet, but I have time to get everything organized."

"We're not far from the border, and British Columbia is beautiful."

"So I've heard. It's also on my list."

The crowd had started to thin, and she wished they could go somewhere and continue their conversation. Instead, he had an early morning start, and her eyelids were getting heavy.

She tipped her head sideways. "What are your plans for this week?"

"I'm starting a big job tomorrow, so I'll need to be at Cohen's collecting supplies as soon as they open."

"That's early. Monday is sometimes my late-start day—seven-thirty."

"Which isn't exactly a late start."

"I know, right. Fortunately I'm a morning person."

She'd stayed put in her seat beside Joel, smiling and nodding at her friends who were filing out of the church.

He seemed content to chat and observe the activity around them. They fell into a comfortable rather than an awkward silence, kind of like when they were out on the water together, rowing or kayaking.

"Will you have time to kayak with me tomorrow after work?" she asked.

"I'm not sure. It depends on the job. I'll message you after lunch with a definite answer."

"No problem." She'd miss Joel's company if he couldn't make her training session.

"What I would love to do is spend a day on the water kayaking the lakes via the rivers." His smile broadened into an enticing grin. "Can we pick a date and make it happen?"

Her pulse quickened, his question switching on her sleepy brain faster than a triple-shot espresso. A date. As in a day and time, or a romantic date? It must be the former, but the part of her that didn't listen to logic or reason longed for the latter. "Sure. I'll need to check my calendar and the weather forecast."

"Of course. It's no fun kayaking in the rain."

She nodded. "Summer rain is fine, but March rain is a different story." Her phone screen woke up and she opened her calendar, ignoring numerous message notifications from Tabby and Leah.

"I was thinking midweek, when you have a day off," Joel said. "I've got some flexibility to juggle my schedule."

"Sounds good. We'll pay attention to the weather and line up a date soon." Was Joel too good to be true? Had she been wearing invisible rose-tinted glasses and missed his obvious flaws? He certainly knew how to charm a girl, and she looked forward to their only-friends kayaking day trip that sounded like it could be a date.

CHAPTER FOUR

Joel slipped on his fitted yellow life vest, clicked the safety buckles in place, and stowed his water bottle in his kayak on the shore of Lake Wainscott. It was a sunny Wednesday morning in late March, and Hannah was satisfied the weather was suitable for Joel's first official tour of the Trinity Lakes and rivers.

Hannah's fluorescent pink vest matched her sleek and distinctive hot pink kayak. Earlier this morning, she'd stored a change of clothes and lunch supplies in Joel's truck, which was now parked by the river on the southern outskirts of town. Their destination was a short walk from the bridge over the river joining the second lake with the smaller Gilbertson Pond in the golf course. He figured the golf course lake was named after someone in Hannah's family. Maybe her father?

Hannah had provided a comprehensive list of supplies to bring, and Joel had protein bars in the zip pockets of his new dry bag. He'd followed her guidelines and worn appropriate clothing and footwear for the expected light breeze and cool conditions on the water.

Hannah placed her dry bag in her kayak. "You ready for the grand tour."

"I can't wait." He pulled his jacket collar higher on his neck, his baseball cap shading his face from the sun.

"Let's do it." Hannah launched her kayak into the water, her ponytail anchoring her pink rowing club cap.

Joel followed Hannah and paddled beside her. The sun warmed his back as they headed west toward town. "What's on our itinerary?"

"We'll start with an easy warm up." Hannah smiled. "The current will pull us toward town."

"Okay." They kayaked close to the southern shore, parallel to Joel's favorite cycling path from the rowing club into town.

"We'll circle back at the bridge," she said.

"Sounds good." The historic stone bridge was in the middle of town.

Joel took gentle and even strokes through the clear blue water, matching Hannah's leisurely pace. Trinity Lakes was a pretty town from the water. The mansions on the hill behind town in the Golf Course Estate shared sweeping mountain and lake views. He absorbed the peace and tranquility, his shoulders relaxing as the current drew them closer to town.

During their training runs, they tended to stick to the eastern section of the lake. They sometimes took a short break on the isolated northern shore near the mountain wilderness area. Uniform rows of fir trees lined the slopes to their east, heading higher into the mountain range.

They reached the bridge and the accompanying bustle in town. Horns honked and engines revved, bringing the small town alive as residents on dry land went about their daily lives.

Hannah pointed to a low-lying dock on the riverbank. "The water level is high from melting snow caps."

"That makes sense. I'd wondered why some of the docks were almost submerged."

"It's a seasonal thing, and one reason why the lake—and the river beyond the bridge—is lined by parkland."

He was glad the town had preserved the parkland. "I like cycling and running on the paths by the shore."

She nodded. "We hold a few cycling and triathlon events during summer. The fresh water is more challenging to swim in than salty ocean water."

"They sound fun."

"Summer in Trinity Lakes is fun. Let's turn around here and go back toward the mountains."

"Sure." Joel was glad he wore sunglasses as they paddled back from the river into the morning sun and the main part of the lake. Traveling against the current, his upper body muscles started getting a workout.

Hannah kayaked beside him, pointing out landmarks and providing a running commentary on the town she loved. He understood the charm and why Trinity Lakes attracted tourists looking to escape the busyness of their lives.

Joel smiled as they passed the familiar rowing club and dock. "Fishing is popular here."

"Especially trout fishing, but it's not my thing."

"It requires patience." He enjoyed fishing from a dock and reading his Bible, reflecting on God's word and praying. All good things.

"Who has time to sit around waiting to catch fish?" She scrunched her nose. "Plus handling fish is yuk."

He raised an eyebrow. "Fresh fish tastes good."

"If someone else catches it, I'm happy to eat it."

He chuckled. "One of my Sydney friends is into ocean fishing. I've been fishing in his motorboat, but I prefer sailing."

"Agreed." Her smile revealed straight white teeth, gleaming in the sunlight. "Dad loved sailing on Sydney Harbour, but this lake is only big enough for dinghy sailing."

"The coast is different to inland lakes." He'd love to drive to

Seattle and sail on Puget Sound during his summer break. "You like dinghy sailing?"

"It's fun, but I prefer Dad's yacht that's moored in Florida."

"Yeah, I would, too." Maybe he could squeeze in a Florida trip later in the year. He'd visit all fifty states if he had more vacation time. "I've heard Florida is great for sailing."

"It is, and cruising on Dad's yacht is more relaxing than dinghy sailing."

He nodded. "Zach, my Sydney friend who owns a yacht, loved sailing in Florida. He'll be visiting Trinity Lakes next week with his wife, Billie."

"How fun that your Aussie friends can vacation here!"

"I can't wait to see them." He appreciated Hannah's enthusiasm and missed his friends back home.

"Have they made plans?"

"They like skiing, but I discovered the mountain resort is closed."

"Skiing finishes by April, and it reopens for summer sports."

"That makes sense." Zach and Billie could ski in Colorado instead. "The plan so far is kayaking, sailing, and cycling."

"I hope the weather is good. They won't need to book ahead for kayaking with us midweek, but I'd recommend contacting the sailing club regarding equipment hire availability."

"Okay. They're staying at Tabby's B&B."

"Tabby will look after them, and they'll probably receive free coffee vouchers for Becky's coffee cart in their welcome package."

"A nice touch." He'd remind his friends to use the vouchers.

"It helps Becky secure tourist trade. Up ahead, we'll cross the lake toward the southern shore."

"Is this where the river splits in two?"

She nodded. "One part flows into this lake, and the other continues on toward the rapids and eventually spills into the other lakes."

"Should I be concerned about the rapids?"

"Not today. It should be calm and more like summer. But I wouldn't take an inexperienced kayaker there today."

"In that case, I'm hoping for an adventure."

She grinned. "You won't be disappointed. Stay behind me, and you can follow my path through the tough parts."

"Will do." Hannah knew these waterways inside out, and he trusted her to find a safe passage through the rough sections.

He followed Hannah's lead, crossing the lake toward the southeastern shore. They paddled to the bend where the lake merged into the river.

She pulled in beside him, letting the current provide them with forward momentum. "I love this section. It's peaceful and relaxing."

"It's stunning, and different to the coastal rivers where I live in Australia."

"Do you have crocodiles?"

He laughed. "Not in Sydney. Crocodiles can be a problem in northern Australia. You don't want to swim or kayak anywhere near them."

"I'll keep that in mind."

"Speaking of dangerous animals, are we likely to come across any bears?" He'd purchased bear spray along with the other essential items on Hannah's list.

"Not here. They'll sometimes go into shallow water to hunt salmon, but they're not like polar bears who can live in the water."

"Phew. That's good to know."

She tipped her head to the side. "You really are concerned about bears."

"Bear spray was on the list. We don't have scary bears back home."

"Your koalas are adorable, and on my must-see list when I visit Australia."

"A good plan, although they're not technically bears."

"They aren't? I'm disappointed."

"They're cute." Like Hannah. He'd reminded himself multiple times that they were friends hanging out, and this kayaking adventure was not a date. Even if it felt like it could be a date. She was in professional tour guide mode and couldn't hide her affection and attachment to her hometown.

He trailed his hand through the cool river water. Too cold for swimming. "I hope you'll visit Sydney and travel around Australia."

"I'd love to vacation there one day."

He nodded. Vacation was an important word to remember. He and Hannah were like cruise ships passing in the night, docking in the same location for a short time. Her life was in Trinity Lakes. He couldn't wait to explore more of the USA and make the most of his vacation year abroad.

They navigated the challenging and fast-moving rapids, and Joel was glad his jacket was waterproof. Before long the serenity of the wilderness was interrupted by the sound of vehicles. A bridge loomed ahead, high above the river.

Hannah pointed to the bridge. "That's the back road from Trinity Lakes, heading to the mountain highway."

"The third bridge."

She nodded. "It's newer than the others, and not exactly pretty, but it does the job and provides a scenic shortcut from town to the ski fields."

"Does that mean we're getting closer to the second lake?"

"The river flows into Lake Other not long after we go under the bridge."

"Huh. Lake Mother." A weird name for a lake.

She snickered. "It's Lake Other, as in the other lake no one cared to name."

"Oh, right." He turned to face her, his voice soft. "I love your accent, but sometimes it trips me up."

Her cheeks flushed and she dipped her head, balancing her paddle across her legs.

Interesting. It looked like he wasn't the only one repeating the we're-just-friends mantra in their mind.

Joel sipped his water and munched on a protein bar. "I guess it's easy paddling from now on."

"It sure is." She stretched out her arms, straightening her spine. "The current will pull us through Lake Other and the river beyond to our lunch stop by the bridge."

"I totally understand why you love your job."

"It's fun to take people on this tour." She beamed a bright smile in his direction. "I'm glad you're enjoying it."

"I am." He was enjoying the tour … and enjoying her company. It was relaxing to escape the daily grind of work and appreciate the quiet beauty of the wilderness.

They reached Lake Other and Hannah pointed to the shore. "There's your summer camp."

"It really is out of town."

She nodded. "The lake's a good size and a short swim to shore."

The summer camp site was large, with room for different activities on land and water. "I imagine capsizing boats and canoes at the camp is common."

"Yeah." Hannah grinned, her face reflecting her fun and fond memories. "Me and Becky usually got wet and muddy."

"Why doesn't this surprise me?" His teasing tone added more color to her face.

"We're strong swimmers and wore vests." She shrugged, as if the thought of staying dry was silly. "No one got hurt."

"That's good. I'm looking forward to volunteering."

"When do you start?"

"Mid-June for three weeks. It should be fun." Now he'd seen the campsite, he couldn't wait to experience his first summer camp.

She widened her grin and picked up her paddle, swinging her kayak closer to him. "I'm sure you'll have a blast."

"I hope so." He looked forward to a break from work in June and spending a chunk of time traveling interstate in July and August. Summer couldn't arrive soon enough.

"I'll show you my favorite camp trick." She reached over and whipped his cap off his head.

"Hey, what are you doing?"

Her cheeky smile revealed a cute dimple. She pulled off her cap and tossed it to him. "We're playing one of my favorite summer camp games."

He ran his fingers over her soft pink cap. "Is this part of the tour guide experience?"

"This is especially for you."

He returned her grin. "Lucky me. How do I win?"

"Whoever throws the cap the longest distance wins the first part, and whoever collects both caps wins the second part."

"What if there's a draw?"

She chuckled. "Welcome to my world. We can win together, rather than losing."

"Okay." He should have guessed Hannah preferred the win-win with no one losing. Her optimism was admirable.

"Joel, ready, set, go." She threw his cap into the air and churned her paddle through the water.

He followed a second behind, and her cap landed further ahead. Part one won, and he raced to overtake her. The current carried the caps at a fast clip, and he reached across Hannah's kayak to snag his cap from the water.

"Joel, we're going to capsize!" She gripped his shoulders, her breath warm on his neck.

"We're not." He pulled her upright and extracted himself from her distracting hug. He stashed his wet cap near his knees and steadied himself in his kayak. "Race you to the next one."

She sped ahead, cutting him off from reaching the cap, and claimed her prize. "I beat you this time."

"A lucky break."

"A winning strategy." She pulled his wet cap out of his kayak and plonked it on his head.

Cool and muddy water, smelling like swamp, trailed down his face and head, seeping under his collar. "You really had to do this."

"Your winning crown. How does it feel?"

He snatched her cap that lay on the front of her kayak, wound his fingers through her silky ponytail, and placed the soggy cap on her head. "It feels like this."

She laughed, a deep, loud, bottom-of-the-belly laugh that was contagious. "I guess I deserved that."

He calmed his own laughter, pulled off his cap and sunglasses, and wiped his face with the back of his hand. "I think you did."

She removed her sunglasses, untangled the cap from her hair, and pulled out the band holding her ponytail. Long wavy locks, highlighted with streaks of caramel and gold in the bright sunlight, and a little bit of mud, spilled around her face and on her shoulders.

He swallowed hard, mesmerized by her beauty and the joy on her face. Words escaped him. He was in too deep, and he couldn't deny the feelings stirring in his heart.

Hannah flicked strands of wet hair back off her face. "I must look like a mess."

He shook his head. "You look beautiful."

Her eyes widened and her mouth opened. "That was the smart answer."

It was the truth. Hannah was a beautiful woman, and he wasn't supposed to be noticing these things. Boy, was he in big trouble.

———

Hannah dragged her gaze away from Joel and placed her sunglasses back on her nose. This moment, in the middle of Lake Other, with swamp scent invading her nostrils, should not rate as a top romantic situation.

She remembered the feel of his taut shoulder muscles that she'd gripped to stay afloat in her kayak, and the intoxicating feeling of being safe within his arms. She had it bad, and she couldn't get Joel out of her mind. And he'd called her beautiful.

She needed time to think and process. "Race you to the bridge."

"You're on." He powered ahead, as if he'd discovered a new source of energy.

Hannah paced herself, settling in a few feet behind him. Her excess emotional energy needed an outlet, and kayaking was her go-to method for reducing stress. She calmed her breathing and prayed for wisdom.

She shouldn't be feeling anything for Joel beyond friendship. Her heart didn't appear to be heeding the memo. He was only in town for part of the year, and his home was thousands of miles away, on the other side of the world.

Joel reached the shore first, and she slid in beside him.

His smile now had the power to flip-flop her heart into a rhythmic gymnastics routine. She needed to get a grip. "Are you hungry?"

"I'm starving and ready for lunch."

"Let's put the kayaks back in your truck and have lunch over there." She indicated a nearby table.

"Sounds like a plan."

She swung into action, found clean towels with her spare clothes in the truck, and shared hand wipes with Joel to clean up and try to eliminate swamp smell.

He placed her picnic hamper on the wooden table, and she

gave him a single serve soup thermos.

"Thanks." He opened the thermos and inhaled. "It smells good."

"I hope you like it." She opened her thermos of homemade hearty veggie soup, full of lentils, beans, and other nutritious ingredients.

He sat opposite at the wooden picnic table, pulling apart a crusty bread roll and dipping it in his soup. "This is delicious. Thank you."

"It's one of my go-to recipes for winter lunches."

"I'm guessing you can make a hearty chicken soup."

She paused. "How'd you know? Is it your favorite?"

He nodded. "I've discovered the fresh soup kits at Leah's store. The fancy chicken soup she sells is awesome."

"I love Leah's soups. I usually make my own and stash the leftovers in the freezer."

"A good idea." His smile crinkled the corners of his eyes. "I'm now a regular at Leah's store."

"I told you that would happen." Joel shared her interest in organic food, and she'd discovered over the last month they had more in common than she'd expected.

Hannah pulled apart her wholegrain bread roll. "Becky has been experimenting with bread making. She baked these rolls last night."

"I didn't know she was a baker."

"It's more of a hobby. She's learning baking skills while working afternoon shifts at the bakery. Her cinnamon rolls are divine but require hours of rowing to burn the calories."

He nodded and leaned forward, his elbows resting on the wooden table slats. "When did you first start rowing?"

She chuckled. "I can't remember. Dad, being the competitive person that he is, had me doing rowing events and interstate meets from when I was in elementary school."

"Did you travel overseas?"

"Many times. A fun way to see the world."

He sipped his soup. "I once went to New Zealand for a rowing meet."

"I'd love to travel there one day."

"It's a great place to visit. My big rowing trip was to England when I was sixteen. It was summer there, and the best part was seeing Wimbledon."

She lifted her chin, meeting his gaze. "I was rowing in England when I was sixteen. Were you at the junior titles?"

He nodded, his eyes widening. "That explains why I recognized you."

"What are the chances?" How could she have forgotten Joel? "It was a big meet."

"It sure was. Your friend, the loud one with purple hair. She was memorable for all the wrong reasons."

A rush of heat flooded her cheeks. "Oh boy, she embarrassed us all. The way she carried on ..."

A wry smile played at the corners of his mouth. "It's all in the past, and I hope she learned from her mistakes. We were only kids."

"True." The good and bad memories filled her mind. Ashlyn from Seattle. Hannah's friend from state meets had made the national junior team with her, and had been boy crazy that summer. Ashlyn's multiple crushes on the cute Aussie boys hadn't ended well. One of those Aussie guys now sat across the table.

Hannah shook her head. "I do remember you. I still can't believe it." Joel was the boy she'd crushed on. They'd talked a couple of times, but Ashlyn's behavior had made everything awkward. "You look different now."

"Nine years will do that." He chuckled, holding her gaze. "Who'd have thought we'd meet again in a different country?"

She nodded, unable to drag her gaze away from the magnetic pull of his eyes. He was a good-looking teen who'd grown into a gorgeous-looking man. Joel was taller, and more muscular than the teen she remembered. "I was so nervous at that meet. It was my first time on the US junior team at an international event."

"Mine, too. The one and only time I represented Australia. I was on the state team at the New Zealand meet, and I quit competition rowing when I finished high school and started my tiling apprenticeship."

"Did you miss rowing?"

He shook his head. "I didn't have time to miss it. My apprenticeship, with the early morning starts, clashed with the team training schedule."

"That's disappointing."

"It made a hard decision easier. Mike, my stepdad, was prepared to sponsor me and provide an allowance if I wanted to continue rowing."

"That must have been a tough option to turn down."

"Yes and no. Rowing was fun, but I wanted to do other things. I had time around my apprenticeship to play sports with friends, and I was happy with my high school achievements."

"That's fair." She could relate to not wanting the professional athlete life.

He turned his head, facing the bridge. "It's a shame we can't continue kayaking into the third lake."

"Trust me, we're not missing anything exciting, other than wayward golf balls using us for target practice. It's a tiny pond compared to the other lakes."

"I'm guessing Gilbertson Pond is named after your dad."

She nodded. "Dad grew up poor, in the less desirable part of town. Back in the day, the golf course he practiced on was nothing like it is now."

"Really? Your dad is self-made?"

"And proud of it. He went to college on a golf scholarship and never looked back."

"Good for him. Small town boy turned sporting hero."

"Yeah, and he achieved his dream of buying the old golf course and creating the country club golf estate." She pointed to the houses on the hill. "Can you see the house with the bright red roof and gables near the top?"

"Next to the house with large windows and a flat roof."

"That's the one. The house below the red roof house is my home."

"Wow, Hannah, you must have spectacular views from your place."

"It's not bad. The best views are from upstairs and my back deck. I feel blessed to live there." And blessed to be spending the day with Joel. She didn't want this day to end.

———

Two days later, Hannah locked her SUV and gave her sister a grim look. "What do think Mom's surprise is?"

"Who knows?" Becky shrugged her shoulders and arms into her denim jacket. "Maybe Mom has a new man in her life?"

"That would be a first." Hannah walked along the path to Mom's front door. There were no unfamiliar cars on the circular drive. "Doesn't look like they're here."

"Yeah." Becky climbed the steps to the porch and pressed the doorbell.

"What's for dinner?" The weekly family get-together was usually held on a Friday evening. Hannah didn't dare avoid Mom's dinner summons unless she had a good reason to explain her absence.

"Grandma's beef stew." Becky tapped her foot on the doorstep.

"That works." Grandma's stew was tasty and nutritious comfort food. Hannah needed comfort when Mom was plotting and scheming.

Grandma opened the door, a wide and welcoming smile on her face. "Please come in. Your mother is upstairs getting ready."

"Getting ready." Becky shook her head. "Why does she need to get ready for a family dinner?"

"The mystery guest." Grandma's eyes twinkled.

"You don't know who it is." Hannah tightened her grip on her purse. It must be a man, for Mom to go to this much trouble to impress a guest.

"She won't tell me. Anyway, why don't you girls give me a hand by setting the table in the dining room? The silverware and dinner set is on the sideboard."

"Sure, Grandma." Why were they using the silver? Mom rarely entertained with the silverware because she claimed it couldn't be put in the dishwasher.

Becky tucked her arm through Hannah's and walked beside her along the hall. "I'm smelling a rat. There's something off about tonight."

"I agree. If she's matchmaking one of us with a friend's son or nephew ..."

"I doubt she'll try that again, after last time."

"I hope you're right." Mom had invited a young man to dinner, the new-to-town nephew of one of her friends. Becky had walked out before the appetizers were served. An awkward meal had followed, and Hannah had made her excuses to leave early when she cleared the dessert plates from the table.

"Are Dan or Leanna in town?" Becky asked.

Hannah shook her head. "Dan's overseas and Leanna messaged me a few hours ago." Mom would be thrilled if Dan was here. She complained that her firstborn avoided visiting her.

"Maybe Mom has finally decided to get over Dad and move on with a new man."

"Who would put up with her?" Mom held onto bitterness

with the same tenacity as a dog chewing a new bone. Could Mom let go of the past and forgive Dad for leaving her?

They worked together to finish setting the table. Grandma arrived with a water jug and chilled sparkling water.

"Your mother bought oysters for our appetizer."

Hannah and Becky shared a glance. Oysters were the appetizer Mom had served on the night Becky walked out.

"Would you like help in the kitchen?" Hannah asked.

"Everything is ready. I need to check the rice, then I'll be back." Grandma left the dining room.

Becky folded her arms across her torso. "I refuse to eat oysters. Mom knows I hate them."

Hannah sighed. "Why can't these dinners be simple?"

"Please distract me from the thought of oysters." Becky closed the dining room door, giving them privacy. "When are you bringing Joel home for dinner with Mom?"

"I'm not bringing Joel, or anyone else, home for dinner. Anyway, we're just friends who spend time together." Her voice held less conviction than last week, and she couldn't stop thinking about her kayaking adventure with Joel.

Becky grinned. "You keep telling yourself that, but I think he's a keeper. He loves my coffee, too."

"Everyone loves your coffee." She blew out a long breath. "I'm worried Mom would say or do something to wreck everything with Joel. If she doesn't like someone, she isn't afraid to let them know."

"Yeah, tact isn't her strong suit."

The doorbell rang. Hannah wrung her hands together. "The moment of truth. Let's go discover who's at the door."

Hannah followed Becky, who walked behind Grandma. Mom beat them to the front door and opened it wide.

"I'm so glad you could make it," Mom's smooth voice echoed in the hall.

A man in a suit stepped inside. Richie.

Hannah's jaw hit the floor and bounced back into place. She stretched her mouth into a polite smile and joined the chorus of welcomes.

"We're so glad you could join us for dinner." Mom smiled, charm oozing from every pore. She wore a chic pants suit, and had styled her wavy blonde-streaked hair into the Farrah Fawcett shag cut she'd worn for as long as Hannah could remember. Artful makeup had removed ten years from her face.

Richie met Hannah's gaze, his eyes lighting up. "I told you we'd catch up for dinner sometime."

She nodded, her lips sealing the inappropriate words itching to escape from the tip of her tongue. Breathe. Think. Plan how to manage the situation.

Mom took control. "Let's move to the dining room. Grandma and I will prepare dinner in the kitchen."

"I insist on helping," Becky said. "Hannah can chat with Richie."

Mom's eyes radiated her approval. "A fabulous idea. We won't be long."

Hannah walked with Richie to the dining room. Becky's disappearing act wasn't helpful, but maybe Hannah could fix the situation with Richie before dinner. "Are you working in town this weekend?"

He nodded. "The clinic was short of doctors, and I volunteered."

"I'm sure they appreciate your assistance, and your family appreciates seeing you."

"It's a win-win." He stepped into the dining room and turned to face her. "I'm also happy to see you tonight."

"About that." Hannah darted around the table to the sideboard. "Would you like still or sparkling water?"

"Sparkling please."

She poured two glasses of sparkling water and handed one to Richie, avoiding his fingertips.

"Thanks." He reached for her hand. "I'm glad we have a moment alone."

She stepped back, removing her hand from his reach by placing it on her hip. "There's no easy way to say this, Richie. My mother has our best interests at heart, but I think of you as my brother's best friend."

His face fell, but he managed a small smile. "There's no hope I can change your mind."

She shook her head. "I've met someone. Mom doesn't know about him."

He raised an eyebrow. "Is it serious?"

"Not yet, but it could be. I'm sorry Mom has given you false hope. I feel like we've been friends forever, and I don't want to ruin our friendship."

Richie nodded. "Thanks for being honest. I'll keep your secret and wish you well."

"Thank you, and I'm glad you understand. We could have a little bit of fun and play along with Mom's silly game."

His mouth curved into a genuine smile. "I value our friendship as well, and I don't want things to become awkward between us."

"Then we're on the same page. We'll act cool around Mom and let her draw her own conclusions."

He nodded. "My mother did warn me that your mother was being pushy." Richie sipped his water. "Mom was concerned you weren't interested in pursuing a relationship."

"Your mom is a sweetheart. Eventually my mother will give up and look for a new victim."

Richie chuckled. "I'm not complaining about the idea of moving off her radar."

Hannah sipped her water, thankful that Richie understood the pressure imposed by Mom's outrageous behavior. Would Mom like Joel? Hannah would do her best to delay Mom meeting Joel for as long as possible.

CHAPTER FIVE

The following week, Joel sat on the dock near the rowing club, waiting for Zach and Billie. A few people were fishing at the end of the dock, and it looked like the fish weren't in a rush to take their bait.

He stretched out his legs, appreciating the sunny Wednesday morning. Earlier he'd stepped inside the rowing club for a few minutes to say hello to Hannah. She was busy, as usual, and he'd left her alone, not wanting to distract her from her work.

But Joel was completely distracted by Hannah. He was glad they'd put together the puzzle pieces and worked out why she looked familiar. If he'd remembered her name, he may have known sooner.

The junior rowing meet in England was an obvious connection. She'd been adorably embarrassed by memories of her friend's crazy and inappropriate behavior. Teenagers were intense, and hard work. His sister was a daily reminder of this reality.

Joel and his teammates had put in a formal complaint to their head coach about the intrusive American girl who wouldn't leave them alone. It was Hannah who had captured

Joel's interest. Not that he would have done anything about his teenage crush on Hannah.

Joel had discovered Hannah shared his faith and lived in a small town on the other side of the world. The few conversations they'd shared, without her annoying friend lurking nearby, had made him wonder if he'd find someone like Hannah back home in Australia.

A few years ago he'd thought he'd found the girl for him. They'd started out as good friends, and hadn't rushed into dating. She'd said she loved him, and he'd believed her feelings were as strong as his own. While he was thinking about engagement rings, she was planning to run away and travel overseas as a missionary without him.

Their breakup was rough, and Zach and Billie had been there for him.

"Joel!" Billie's loud voice carried from the shore.

He turned around, smiling. It was great to see his Aussie friends and hear their accents. He caught up with Zach and Billie near the entrance to the rowing club.

Billie gave Joel a hug and Zach and Joel shared a fist bump.

"Are you ready to kayak?" Joel asked.

Zach shook his head. "Billie has something important to do first."

"Joel, why didn't you mention I can get a genuine Aussie meat pie here?" Billie grinned, bobbing on her heels.

"From Becky's coffee cart or the bakery in town?"

She raised her eyebrows. "A bakery has them, too?"

"I didn't know you were a fan." He couldn't remember Billie eating a meat pie.

"After almost four months away from home, I'm desperate for anything Aussie."

Zach laughed. "You're making it sound like our overseas holiday is a prison sentence."

Billie swatted her husband's arm with her baseball cap. "I've loved our time away, but I'll be ready to fly home next month."

"It's a hard life, Billie." Joel grinned. "How many states have you visited?"

Zach began counting fingers, then stopped as if he were counting in his head. "Thirteen at last count."

"Has Bek settled into college life in Kansas?" In August last year, Zach's younger sister had surprised everyone by hopping on a plane to go and study at a small-town Bible college.

Billie nodded. "She's gone dark on social media and is calling herself Becky these days."

"She doesn't look like a Becky." Joel couldn't figure out why Bek would change her name. She'd always introduced herself as Bek, or Rebekah.

"We agree, and we're still calling her Bek." Zach switched his attention to a sailing boat departing from the dock adjacent to the sailing club. "I think the name change is temporary."

"Bek's studying and working behind the scenes on an Easter Passion Play." Billie paused, turning to Joel, and lowering her voice. "And she's met a nice American guy."

"Really? What's he like?" Bek's ex-boyfriend had been a piece of work—a ruthless gold digger who Bek had dumped when she discovered his real intentions.

"He's a farm mechanic and wears a cowboy hat." Billie rolled her eyes. "He's not the type of guy we'd expected her to date."

"Bek is dating a cowboy. For real." Joel couldn't picture Bek with a cowboy.

"Yeah." Zach rubbed his hand over his jaw. "I can't see my sister happily living on a farm or a ranch in the middle of nowhere."

Billie sighed. "True love can conquer all. And speaking of love, I'm looking forward to meeting your Hannah."

Joel shook his head. "She's not my Hannah."

"She might be, soon." Billie chuckled. "We're praying you'll make smart decisions."

"Thanks. Your prayers mean a lot." He'd made friends at the college, but it wasn't the same as being with his friends back home.

"Trust me, Joel." Her tone switched from lighthearted to serious. "I'll chat with Hannah and make sure she's on the level."

"Okay." There was no point arguing with Billie. She was like a mother hen, and she'd asked him dozens of questions when she'd first heard about Hannah. He appreciated that Billie cared enough to want to get to know Hannah.

Billie clapped her hands together. "Who wants a meat pie before we head out?"

"I'm in," Joel said. "Becky's coffee is excellent, too."

Zach nodded. "We discovered this earlier, and it's hit and miss finding good coffee."

"Becky's coffee is always a hit." Joel walked with his friends toward Becky's coffee cart. "The Bellbird Café in town is another good option. They have Aussie food on their menu."

"Yay for real Aussie food." Billie fell into step between Joel and Zach. "We can go there for lunch today."

"That works. I'll show you around the Bible college after lunch, before Zach's meeting."

"A great idea." A truckload of enthusiasm infused Zach's words.

Zach had visited numerous Bible colleges during their travels. Listening to Billie, it didn't sound like she'd be happy to relocate for Zach to study overseas. Joel would need to navigate the relocation issue with Hannah if they wanted to pursue a relationship.

Joel placed his order and chatted with Becky while she made their coffee. They collected their pies and coffee and headed back to an outdoor table at the rowing club.

He slid into a bench seat and waved hello to Gracie, who'd

collected Hannah's coffee mug and was on her way to see Becky. He'd messaged Hannah, who said she'd stop by to see them when she took her break.

He sipped his cappuccino and took his time eating his pie while Zach and Billie talked about their travel adventures. Hannah soon wandered over, coffee in hand.

"Hey." Joel made the introductions and appreciated the warm greetings Hannah received from his friends.

Hannah smiled and shuffled onto the bench beside him. "I hope you're enjoying visiting my town."

Billie glanced around, her smile wide. "I love it here, and the lake is beautiful. A hidden gem, and a nice change of pace from busy touristy places."

Hannah nodded. "You're here at a good time. Weekends and summer are crazy busy."

Billie was tactful in her choice of conversation topics, disguising her probing questions. He anticipated hearing a detailed appraisal from Billie later.

Joel polished off his cappuccino and turned to Hannah. "I'll follow you inside and make the arrangements for the kayaks."

"Sure. I have three ready in the shed, plus everything else you've requested."

"Thanks," Joel said. "We appreciate it."

Hannah's warm smile encompassed the group. "You're welcome to use the club facilities. There's refreshments available and shower facilities, if needed."

Zach nodded. "Thanks for the offer."

"You're welcome." Hannah stood. "Enjoy your time on the lake."

"We will," Billie said.

Joel walked with Hannah toward the boat shed.

"I'm glad your friends are enjoying their vacation."

"Me, too. After kayaking, we're going into town for lunch at the Bellbird. Do you have any plans tonight?"

She shook her head. "I'll hit the gym after work."

"Would you like to join us in town for dinner?"

"Sure." She opened one of the boat shed roller doors. "Which restaurant?"

"We haven't picked one yet. You can help us decide."

"That I can do."

"Sounds good." He held her gaze. "I can swing by your place and give you a lift."

They usually traveled separately. His suggestion was practical, but was nudging things a little bit outside their comfortable-friends zone.

Hannah's smile lit up her face. "A ride sounds good. I'll message you my address."

"I think I drove past your place yesterday, on my way to a job. Assuming you're across the road from the red roof house."

She nodded. "It's a distinctive landmark."

"It sure is." Hannah's home, situated in the exclusive Trinity Lakes Golf Course Estate, was only a short walk from the entrance to the country club. He'd discovered the mansions further up the hill, where his job was located, were luxurious, sprawling over large blocks of land.

"I'm looking forward to dinner," Hannah said. "Zach and Billie are nice people."

"They're good friends." Like his Aussie friends, Hannah was down to earth and didn't have an entitled attitude that could be born from a life of privilege. She was prepared to do menial work and be a team player. He was falling for her, yet he didn't know if they could have a future together.

———

THE NEXT MORNING, Hannah rode her bicycle along the riverfront and under the stone bridge in town. She'd arranged to meet Joel at the sailing club and cycle with him while Zach and Billie were sailing.

Hannah continued along the wide path toward her rowing club, glad to see people were out and about enjoying the sunshine. The warmer weather and early sunrises provided opportunities for Hannah to cycle to and from work. She preferred outdoor cycling to riding stationary bikes at the gym. The downhill stretch from home was easy, although she'd feel the pain in her leg muscles when she rode home up the steep hill.

The light breeze provided ideal conditions for outdoor sports. She spotted Joel up ahead, his bike leaning against a picnic table. Last night she'd shared a fun dinner with him and his friends at the local Italian restaurant. They'd laughed all evening, and she'd learned a lot about Joel's life and friends in Australia.

Sydney sounded like an awesome city to visit, with plenty of water-sports opportunities. Joel lived near a tidal ocean lagoon connected to a beach. She'd learned his home was high enough above sea level to not be impacted by floodwaters.

She rode past the old boat shed. If the rumors circulating around town were true, the old boat shed and surrounding land across the road from Tabby's B&B was owned by a trust that was somehow connected to one of Tabby's relatives. How the lakefront land had been zoned as a floodplain was a mystery. It didn't make sense that the zoning change was made in error. Hannah's father was an astute businessman, and the current zoning devalued their land by halting development opportunities.

Hannah should bump investigating the land zoning arrangements higher on her to-do list. With summer coming, she had plenty of more important work to do at the rowing club. She hoped Tabby's family could confirm the rumors were true, and then discover the logical reasons behind the land zoning change.

Joel waved and Hannah slowed her bike, stopping near his table. She removed her bike helmet and attached the helmet straps around the handlebars. Her plaited hair fell forward over her shoulder.

"Sorry to keep you waiting," she said.

"It's all good. Zach and Billie only left the dock a few minutes ago."

"Okay." He covered his mouth, as if he was hiding a yawn. "I had a slow start this morning and slept through my alarm."

"I slept in too, and drove here with my bike in the back of my truck."

She grinned. "Last night was fun. Thanks for inviting me."

"Zach and Billie loved spending time with you. We stayed out later than I'd planned."

"Yeah. I'm getting too old to do late nights and not suffer for it."

Joel laughed. "You and me both. I'm glad we did."

"So am I." She admired Joel's athletic build, highlighted by his snug fitting cycling jersey over loose fitting shorts. "Have you had your morning coffee? We could stop by Becky's first, if we have time."

"I always have time for Becky's coffee." He pointed to a boat on the far side of the lake. "They'll be sailing for a few more hours."

"It's a nice day for it."

"Zach is happy."

She nodded and wheeled her bike alongside Joel's. They crossed the road to Becky's usual spot in the RV park and left their bikes near a table in the shade.

Her sister gave them a big smile from behind the counter. "It's coffee time, or are we eating before burning the calories?"

Joel chuckled. "Only a small cappuccino for me. I'm ignoring your amazing cinnamon rolls today."

"That's a shame," Becky said. "I helped the baker make this batch yesterday afternoon, and they taste so good."

Hannah pursed her lips. "I shouldn't … I really shouldn't, but can you please put one aside to take home for me later."

He drew his eyebrows together. "You're changing our route and making me ride into the mountains."

"Would you mind?" She gave him her most cajoling smile. "I'm feeling like I need a long calorie-burning hill climb, followed by a treat." Last night they'd agreed to forego the mountain climb for a long ride along the flat paths beside the lake and river before meeting Zach and Billie for lunch.

Becky snickered. "Joel, I can always put two cinnamon rolls aside, and you can stop by our place to collect them."

"She has a point." Hannah held his gaze. "We can go easy on the butter and have herbal tea."

He laughed. "Because herbal tea makes everything healthy in Hannah's world. I know the drill."

Becky joined in, laughing along. "I'm bagging two cinnamon rolls and making your coffee."

"Thanks, Becky." She contained her own laughter and turned to Joel. "If we cycle up the long hill into the mountains, we can cruise downhill into town and put the bikes in the back of your truck."

He shook his head. "I know the truth. You don't want to ride home up the hill after lunch when you're feeling tired."

"You got it." She'd ride to and from work more often if she didn't have to climb that hill home after a long day of work.

Joel collected their coffees from Becky, and they settled in the folding chairs under a shady tree.

She sipped her small latte. "We can stop by my place later today."

"That could work. Zach has another appointment at the Bible college after lunch."

"Is he planning on studying in Trinity Lakes?" She hadn't picked up on that thread of information at dinner when they'd discussed Bible colleges.

"He's investigating all his options. I suspect if he does eventually do it, he'll go to Bible college in Australia."

"Okay. Why don't we have hot tea with the rolls for afternoon tea? See, I'm learning your lingo."

He gave her a thumbs up. "You're doing great, and lunch with Zach and Billie is all organized."

"What's for lunch?"

"A picnic hamper should arrive at the sailing club at one."

She clapped her hands together. "That sounds fun, followed by a cinnamon roll later."

He sipped his coffee. "Are you sure you don't want to eat it now?"

"No, I'm good. I'll be starving after our ride."

"Won't we all. Billie and Zach will be ready for lunch after sailing, too."

"They're a cute couple, and sailing dates are so romantic." She widened her eyes, realizing she'd spoken her thoughts aloud. Dinner last night had felt like a double date. They'd danced around the whole are-we-dating-or-not routine, and now she'd put the previously unspoken words front and center.

Joel placed his hand over hers on the table, his touch gentle and caring. "Would you like to go on a sailing date, followed by lunch somewhere nice?"

She nodded and held his warm gaze. "Yes, I'd like that."

Hannah loved the idea of a sailing date, and exploring possibilities with Joel as they took small steps outside the friend zone into new territory.

———

JOEL PUSHED HARD on his bike pedals, relieved to see a road sign ahead indicating the turn off to the mountain lookout. He followed Hannah, pain shooting through his legs as he cycled along the dirt path. His muscles burned from the long and steep hill climb. He slowed to a halt beside a bench seat.

He stumbled onto the seat, legs wobbly and feeling like jelly. He'd been crazy to let Hannah talk him into doing this ride. Was a cinnamon roll worth it? Maybe not, but Hannah was definitely worth it. She'd said yes to his sailing date, and she'd received Billie and Zach's stamp of approval.

Hannah had collapsed on the bench seat beside him, eyes closed, breathing rapid, and perspiration beading on her skin. Her natural beauty distracted him from his own discomfort.

He deepened his breathing, filling his lungs with much-needed oxygen. The crisp mountain air, an earthy scent with a hint of pine, cooled his heated face and body.

He reached for his water bottle in the drink holder clipped onto his bike frame. He drank small sips, quenching his thirst and hydrating his body. He'd need to start moving and stretching soon to flush the lactic acid from his muscles.

"How are you feeling?" He met Hannah's weary gaze. "We need to stretch."

"My legs are burning." She sipped her water, shifting her gaze to the view over the valley and Trinity Lakes. "I could sit here all day and stare at this view."

He stood and looked down into the valley. Lake Wainscott glistened below, the golf course estate hill a prominent landmark near the town and lake. "We can enjoy the view on the downhill run."

"If only the trees didn't hide most of it."

"Yeah." He jogged on the spot, his muscles sore. "It would have been easier to drive here."

"This ride is nostalgic. In high school we jogged or cycled

the lower section of the mountain road as part of our fitness program."

He chuckled. "Hill runs are not my favorite."

"Dan used to bribe me into running or cycling all the way up here." She stood and stretched, copying Joel's movements. "My brother needed a training partner, and no one else would do it."

No surprise there. "What was the reward? I imagine it must have been good."

She nodded and sipped her water. "He'd take me and one of my friends for a day's shopping in Spokane. We'd sometimes catch a movie, too."

"He was brave, taking teenage girls shopping. My sister Bella takes forever to find what she wants at the mall."

"Richie, his best friend, would often tag along."

"Is this the Richie I've met?"

She nodded. "Richie has been my friend for years, since elementary school. He was also on the rowing team."

Interesting. Hannah shared a closer history with Richie than he'd realized. "Was Richie in England at the meet?"

"No. He was a college freshman with a rowing scholarship by then." She turned and stared into his eyes, her gaze solemn. "Mom would like me to date Richie, but it's not going to happen."

He gulped. "Does Richie know this?" When he'd met Richie at the rowing club, Richie had seemed determined to become a bigger part of Hannah's life.

"I wasn't going to mention this, but I guess I should in case Becky or Grandma says something." Her tone was flatter than the pancake he'd eaten for breakfast.

"Okay." He looked away and placed the heel of his foot on the bench seat, moving into a stretch. Would he need time to absorb and process her bad news?

"Last weekend, Mom surprised us by inviting Richie to our family dinner."

Wow. Hannah wasn't wrong when she'd mentioned her mother liked matchmaking. "How'd it go?"

"It was awkward, but I talked to Richie, and we're still friends."

"A good outcome." An excellent outcome from Joel's perspective. One less rival for Hannah's affections.

"I guess so." She grabbed a towel from her bike bag. "I'm looking forward to changing out of these sweaty clothes before lunch."

"Me, too." He had spare clothes in his truck. The shower facilities were a convenient benefit of his rowing club membership.

She stretched her toned arms above her head. Wisps of hair had escaped from her plaits and frizzed into adorable curls.

He followed her lead, the muscle burn easing. "We'll need to check our work schedules—and the weather—to pick a day for sailing."

"It could be tricky with the rain that's forecast."

"I can wait." Their sailing date would mark a turning point in their relationship. He'd find time to plan the perfect day and organize lunch for two after a fun morning on the water. There was no turning back, and he prayed Hannah would love their first official date.

CHAPTER SIX

A few weeks later, Hannah refilled her water bottle in the rowing club kitchen and placed it next to her phone and dry bag on a nearby table. The weather was beautiful and perfect for sailing. Joel had booked their sailing date for late morning, and Tabby had agreed to start at eleven to cover Hannah's shift.

It was a treat to take time off on a Wednesday afternoon plus Thursday and Friday. Joel's work schedule was hectic and didn't allow him time away that coordinated with her roster. Tabby was unavailable on weekends, and already working long hours between her job here and the B&B.

Hannah ducked into her office and collected her pink vest from the hook inside the door. Since Zach and Billie's visit, Hannah had seen Joel a couple of afternoons for outdoor rowing training, and at church on Sunday evenings. Easter had come and gone in a whirl of activity, along with spring break. Joel's reputation as an excellent tiler had spread, and he'd been too busy with work in town to stop by for lunch on her quieter weekdays at the rowing club.

She returned to the kitchen area and looked around. Had she forgotten anything?

Tabby walked into the clubhouse, a bright smile on her face. "I made it on time."

"I appreciate you." She placed her vest on the chair beside her bag.

"No problem." Tabby put a few food containers in the fridge. "I managed to get everything done at the B&B, plus pack my lunch."

"I'm glad it worked out." She sat at the table and stored her drink bottle in a dry bag pocket. "Please make sure you take a lunch break."

"Will do. When are you meeting Joel?"

Hannah glanced at the clock on the wall. "In fifteen minutes. He's making the arrangements. All I have to do is turn up."

"It's so romantic." Tabby switched on the electric kettle and placed a tea bag in her mug. "I knew from the start, when he joined the club and kept turning up in the afternoon to train with you, that something was bound to happen."

Hannah smiled and squashed the embers of fear that lingered in her mind. "Today is a big step, our first official date. I think we're leaving the friend zone."

"I'm happy for you. I can't remember the last time I had a date with something other than a good book."

"What about your handsome houseguest? Has he asked you out yet?" Hannah had noticed the houseguest discreetly watching Tabby. He was interested, and he looked like Tabby's type.

"Logan doesn't think of me like that. Besides, he's not a Christian."

Disappointment crushed her hopes. If only he was a believer. "Faith is important, and I'm glad Joel is a Christian. I'm praying God will have someone for you."

"I know, and I'm praying I can be content, whatever my

circumstances. Sometimes I feel like I'm spinning my wheels, going nowhere, and life is passing me by."

Hannah tapped her fingers on the tabletop. "Finding contentment is hard. I don't know if I have a future with Joel. My life is here, in Trinity Lakes. Maybe I'm selfish, but I'm reluctant to consider the prospect of changing my life for a guy."

"I understand. Change can be scary." Tabby poured hot water into her mug.

"Yep." Hannah stood and slipped her hot pink vest over her waterproof jacket. "Book club is tomorrow night. Have you finished reading Ghost Heart?"

"Almost. I do like medical thrillers."

"It was a good one, and I want to read more in the series." Hannah had previously read romantic suspense books by Lisa Harris. Her co-author, Lynne Gentry, was a new author who Hannah had added to her long must-read-again author list.

"I'm glad we started with book one. Before I forget, I have some news on the floodplain zoning issue."

"Really? You have answers already?" It was still on Hannah's to-do list to investigate the questions Tabby had raised. Hannah's trust fund documentation, which included the land transfer from her father, didn't specify why the flood zoning existed or how it had happened.

"Not yet, but we've hired an expert to find the answers." Tabby shared the details on who they'd hired and why it was necessary.

Hannah tipped her head to the side. "Will they need to do a formal investigation, and write a report for the town?"

"It's a possibility, depending on what records they can dig up."

"It's sounding like a complicated process." Since the zoning impacted Hannah's land in her trust fund, she may need to consider hiring someone to independently investigate Tabby's questions. The sailing club buildings on her land were small, and there was vacant land closer to the road that could be built on to expand the sailing club. It was a low-priority issue to discuss with her father.

She picked up her phone and added a note to follow this up in May or June when Dad next visited Trinity Lakes.

Tabby leaned back against the counter and sipped her tea. "Gran always told me she'd wanted to turn the old boatshed into a wedding venue. I guess she must have known about the zoning."

"Maybe." If Dad knew about the zoning, then other business owners probably knew, too.

Hannah picked up her dry bag. "I've sent you an email that includes a list of jobs. It's a short list, and it should be an easy afternoon."

"Sounds good. Say hi to Joel from me, and enjoy your date."

"Will do, and I'm looking forward to it." Hannah tucked her phone in her pocket and headed outdoors, ready to meet Joel at the sailing club.

It was two months since Joel had first visited the rowing club to do the quote. During that time, he'd gained Hannah's trust and become an important part of her life.

Hannah was thankful she'd jumped early and had her tiling work done last month. Now, Joel was booked through April and May, with a wait list. His boss at the construction company wanted to recruit another tiler to reduce the backlog.

She found Joel on the sailing club dock, loading supplies into what looked like a fifteen-foot dinghy.

He waved, a broad smile covering his tanned face.

She returned his wave and walked the length of the wooden dock to the boat mooring. Her sunglasses were in her bag somewhere, and she'd need them to block the glare from the sparkling water.

"Hey, do you need any help?" she asked.

"We're good to go." He held out his hand. "I'll take your bag, then help you onboard. These dinghies like to bob around."

"They sure do." Hannah passed over her gear, and then placed her hand in his. A jolt of awareness shot through her, and she was glad to have an excuse for wobbly legs. Weak knees were a real possibility.

He tipped his sunglasses up on top of his baseball cap and met her gaze. "I'm happy you said yes to sailing."

"So am I." She stepped into the boat, his gorgeous eyes reeling her in. Their attraction was strong, and she leaned in, closing the distance between them.

His gaze dropped lower, to her mouth. The water shifted under the boat, buckling her knees, and knocking her sideways. She steadied her feet, he gripped her elbows, and the moment was lost.

She groaned. "Um, I think I need to work on my balance."

"Yeah, falling overboard isn't ideal." His teasing tone added more heat to her flushed face.

"It's really not." Hannah was determined to stay in the boat and focus on sailing. Why had she thought this was romantic?

She'd better stop being distracted by Joel and concentrate on the task at hand. She found her sunglasses buried in her bag. Teamwork was essential if they wanted to make the most of their time cruising around Lake Wainscott.

The fickle and frequent wind direction changes kept her mind on the job, and away from the botched almost-kiss. Even in the romcom movies it was usually an external distraction, rather than a klutzy heroine, that ruined the moment.

She followed Joel's instructions, ducking under the boom, moving around the cockpit, and adjusting the sail ropes to maintain their fast pace. Who needed a motorboat when they could tack at a moment's notice, and catch all the beneficial wind changes?

"Have you raced dinghies?" she asked.

"I sure have." He stood at the helm, steering the boat. "It's a lot of fun."

"Yeah, and it's all coming back to me." She'd found her sea legs and fallen into the familiar sailing routines she'd learned during her high school and college years.

He lowered his cap over his face. "When did you last sail on this lake?"

"A few years ago." She declined to mention she'd turned down several sailing date invitations, including a couple with a more-than-friends vibe from Richie. She was glad she'd had the conversation at Mom's with Richie to clear the air, and the awkwardness had passed. Mom hadn't given up on Richie, and he'd been sweet in how he handled Mom's interfering ways.

"Are you a member of the sailing club?" he asked.

"No, but I could join. My trust fund owns the land and leases the property to the club."

"Okay. That explains a few things."

"What do you mean?" Joel had never shown any interest in her financial situation, and she was aware he had enough money to live comfortably. It was a matter of public record that her trust fund included the RV park, camping ground, and a swath of lakefront land.

"After I mentioned your name, they gave me a larger boat and a bigger discount."

She nodded. "I'm glad they did. I've been offered honorary membership."

"You haven't considered accepting their offer?"

"I work weekends when the members do their racing. I don't have time to fit in sailing."

"That makes sense. You're busy, and it took weeks to coordinate our schedules for today."

"True, and now Easter and spring break have passed, we're moving into the peak summer tourist season."

"I'm glad I could see you more often over Easter."

"Me, too. A few people in town wanted me to open on Good Friday and Easter Sunday for the tourists, but that's a line in the sand I'm not prepared to cross."

"Good for you." He steered the boat closer to the northern shore. "People can enjoy the lake in their own boats and kayaks."

"That's always been my argument. The rowing club isn't an essential service. Plus, my team likes having a break at Easter."

"I get it, and I still find it weird that Good Friday is like a normal workday. In Australia, nearly everything is closed."

"Funny you say that. It would be closed here, too, if some people had gotten their way."

"Really?" He circled the boat around before they reached the stone bridge in town. "It sounds like there's a story to tell."

Hannah switched seats and tightened her ponytail to secure her baseball cap. "Years ago, when the first of the Aussie families settled here, there was a big push to close for three days at Easter, including Saturday. I remember Dad talking about it, and how the town was divided on the issue."

"How interesting. Their push was only for three days."

"I think so. Why?"

"In most parts of Australia, Easter is a four-day public holiday weekend from Friday to Monday."

"An extra-long weekend. It would be nice to have a four-day holiday weekend, and more time to reflect on Jesus and the importance of Easter."

He nodded. "In Sydney, like here, Easter usually falls during the school holiday break, and we have our big Easter show event running at the same time."

"That sounds fun." Spring break was an ideal time to hold a fair. "Do you have rides and animals? Is there a rodeo, or a parade?"

"Not exactly a rodeo, but it's a similar atmosphere to a parade with amusement park rides and show bags. It's when the country comes to the city with their prize-winning animals and produce."

She grinned. "I'd love to visit your Easter show."

"Maybe one day you could visit Australia for Easter."

"I hope so." She ducked under the boom and switched to the bench seat opposite. "The more we talk, the more I realize how different your life in Australia is compared to here."

He pointed to the sun overhead. "It's in the wrong position, for starters. I'm still confusing north and south."

"That's something I hadn't considered."

"Our seasons are opposite, with Christmas in summer."

"Yeah, that's confusing." She had trouble conceptualizing hot summer weather in December. "I have interstate coaching commitments during our summer."

"It's great you can travel for work."

"I enjoy it, and the teens are available to work more when school is out." The rowing club would be busy every day, and open long hours from sunrise to sunset.

"Are you planning to take any time off over summer?"

She shook her head. "I'll work through until school goes back. Maybe squeeze in a vacation in September or October, and visit Dad."

"In Florida?"

"It depends. Hurricane season can make it tricky. Last year we vacationed in Europe. Sometimes we go to Hawaii." Dad usually made their vacation plans at the last minute. She'd suggested an Alaskan cruise via Canada if there were bookings available.

"I'll have to start calling you Miss Jet-setter."

She laughed. "Says the man from the land Down Under."

"Don't knock it till you visit. Are you ready to head into shore for lunch?"

"I'm famished, after all this hopping around the boat."

"Good. I've booked a table at the Bellbird."

"Sounds great." The Bellbird Café was Joel's favorite, and their usual venue for book club. She looked forward to lunch with great food and great company.

———

JOEL PULLED out a chair for Hannah at a window table in the Bellbird Café, overlooking Main Street. He didn't need a menu to select his order. Hannah took her time, pondering the menu items and daily specials.

"What do you feel like?" he asked.

"Everything looks good, and it's hard to make a decision."

"A good problem to have." The cafe had grown on him, with its mismatched tables and chairs, and old-fashioned china cups and plates displayed on yellow walls. Birdsong background music softened the footsteps on wooden floorboards.

"Okay." She met his gaze. "I'll have the chicken parma, plus a cappuccino."

"Ah, the parmy." It was interesting how the American abbreviation for parmigiana was different to his version. Ordering food was complicated.

She lifted an eyebrow. "Parmy. That's a new-to-me Aussie word."

He grinned. "Add it to your list, and I'll place our order."

"I will, and thanks." She reached for her phone and tapped the screen alive. "While you do that, I'll check in with Tabby."

"No worries." The rowing club was in good hands when Tabby was in charge. He made his way to the counter, placed their order, and chatted with one of the owners, who'd guessed Joel was on a date. There was nowhere to hide any secrets in Trinity Lakes now the residents had embraced him as one of their own.

Ten minutes later, a server placed two cappuccinos on their table. The sweet coffee aroma ratcheted up his hunger pangs.

He should have eaten a bigger breakfast this morning, but he'd been nervous about their date.

Hannah sipped her cappuccino. "I see you're a regular."

"What gave me away?"

"Not looking at a menu."

"Guilty as charged. I eat here a lot with the college guys, or we order takeout." The Bible college provided onsite meal options, including kitchen facilities, but he liked to support the businesses in town by regularly dining in their restaurants.

"It's good you've made friends at the college."

"They're a fun group, dedicated to their studies." He'd introduced Hannah to a few of the guys, and she'd seen his dorm, and toured the facilities.

"It's good they're into sports, like you."

"Yeah, we've been training for the upcoming AFL match."

"Oh, you mean the Anzac football game?"

He nodded. "Are you working that day?"

"Yes." She stirred the milky foam in her cup. "I always miss the Anzac game because it's held on a Saturday."

"I get it, but I'm disappointed. I'd hoped you'd cheer me on from the sideline."

Her beautiful smile widened. "I'm sure you'll be fine and play well."

"AFL isn't my best ball sport, and I'm hoping it goes well."

"There's usually video footage floating around after the game. I can catch the highlights."

"Highlights are okay, but it's not the same as watching live or being at the game." The time differences meant he rarely watched live sport from Australia. A small sacrifice for the experience of working and living overseas.

She finished her coffee and tipped her head to the side. "Do you ever feel homesick and wish you were back in Australia?"

He nodded. "Mum can pull on my heartstrings, and I think she misses me more than she's willing to admit."

"I'm sure she does."

A server appeared with their lunch. His steak with mushroom sauce looked and smelled amazing, with curly fries and veggies on the side.

He placed his hand over hers. "I'll say grace."

"Thank you." She threaded her fingers through his and closed her eyes.

He shut his eyes and said a short prayer, her hand feeling like it belonged in his. He was thankful for their date and for this window of uninterrupted time together.

Hannah's wide eyes matched her smile. "My chicken parma —I mean parmy—looks delicious. Thanks for lunch."

"You're welcome." His first mouthful of tender beef hit the spot. The Bellbird was an excellent pick for their lunch date.

"This is good." Hannah's face expressed her delight. "I'm guessing you're close to your mom."

He nodded. "It was just the two of us for a few years after my parents split. Dad didn't fight for custody, which made a horrible situation less painful."

"Your parents were smart."

"They may have been smarter if they'd stayed together, but it is what it is. Who am I to judge?"

"Good point. Did you see your dad often after they split?"

"In the school holidays." Dad had prioritized taking leave from work to spend quality time with him. "He remarried and moved to Adelaide a few years after Mum remarried."

"That's a lot of changes."

"Yeah, especially after Bella and Jack were born. Mum and I stayed close. Mike has always traveled with work." Mum had complained about Mike's frequent work trips, but Mike had been based in Sydney until this year.

She stared into his eyes, her empathy reaching him across the table. "Do you get along with Mike?"

"We're very different people, but I know he cares despite how he can come across. Bella clashes with him, big time."

Her eyes widened a fraction. "That's not fun."

"It really isn't. Part of the problem is they're too much alike, and they're both stubborn." Mum was worried about Bella. All he could do, from the other side of the world, was pray for his family.

Hannah sipped her water. "Mom is stubborn, and she wouldn't have coped if Dad had tried to push for custody."

"Was their divorce messy?"

Hannah dabbed her mouth with her napkin. "Sadly, messy is too mild a description."

"I'm sorry, Hannah."

"Yeah." She lowered her lashes, her voice wavering. "Mom made some wild accusations, and claimed to have evidence that proved Dad was a bad person."

"Oh man, that would have put you and your siblings in the middle."

She pressed her lips together, looking like she was struggling with the memories. "It was horrible, and Grandma helped us cope with everything."

He reached across the table and placed his hand on hers. "It's a blessing you have Gracie's love and support." Gracie was the grandma everyone wanted to adopt. Her granddaughters had inherited her big heart.

Hannah nodded. "There's a reason I haven't introduced you to my mother."

His jaw fell slack. "You don't think she'll like me." Gracie and Becky had welcomed him with open arms into Hannah's life, and so had the Trinity Lakes community.

"It's not personal, Joel."

He withdrew his hand and picked up his water glass. "It kind of feels that way." It sounded like he'd no chance of winning over Hannah's mother.

Her eyes reflected her frustration and pain. "No one is good enough for Mom, not even the doctors she tries to force me to date." She stabbed her fork into a curly fry on her plate.

He sliced his steak into bite sized pieces. "What's the deal with the doctors?"

She took her time answering. "Her father, my grandfather, was a surgeon. My theory is Mom thinks a doctor would make a good husband."

He shook his head, chewing on the tasty beef and her hard to swallow words. Susannah Gilbertson's logic didn't add up. An occupation didn't define a person's ability to love and care for a family. "I'm sorry you have to deal with her attitude."

She shrugged, regaining her composure, and pulling on her brave face. "I'm used to it, and I try not to think about it. I can't change the situation or make it better."

He admired her inner strength and her willingness to share her emotional pain. "I understand, but I'm a little confused. Did your mother provide evidence to back up her allegations about your father?"

"We don't know what the truth is, or if any real evidence ever existed." She let out a soft sigh. "When Dan pushed Mom for details, she refused to talk."

Wow. "My parents' breakup was hard, but it sounds like it was a lot easier to manage than what you've experienced."

She nodded. "Dad isn't perfect. No one is, other than Jesus. I'm sure Dad made mistakes and did things he regrets. Mom is difficult to manage."

"Did your dad have any custody when you were younger?"

"Only occasionally, during our vacation time." She sipped her water. "The weird thing was Dad traveled most of the year, and we didn't notice him missing in many ways because he was hardly at home before they got divorced anyway."

Who could blame her father for staying away? Joel would brace himself for his first meeting with Hannah's mother.

Susannah Gilbertson was known around town for being diffi-cult and hard to please. People wondered how Wayne Gilbertson had coped being married to Susannah for so many years.

Hannah finished her chicken and placed her napkin on the table. "Now you know my family baggage, are you still inter-ested in dating me?"

He grinned. "Of course I am."

She let out a long breath. "I had dreaded talking to you about Mom."

"All families have problems. Bella is being difficult and getting into trouble."

"I'm sorry to hear that." Hannah topped up the water in her glass. "How old is she?"

"Fourteen." A difficult age, according to Mum. He popped a curly fry in his mouth.

A family of four with two teen daughters walked by and sat together at a table on the far side of the cafe. The girls pulled out their phones, their eyes glued to the screens. Several minutes ticked by and the girls continued to ignore the adults at their table, oblivious to their surroundings. His sister was the same. Secretive and uncommunicative with Mum.

He focused on finishing his meal and pondered his sister's situation. "Bella's friends aren't the best influence on her."

Hannah placed her glass on the table. "Peer pressure isn't fun. I'll pray for her."

"Thank you. I'll be praying for your family, too."

"We'll need all your prayers, with Mother's Day coinciding with Mom's birthday next month."

He nodded. That weekend would be tricky to navigate. "Does this mean your family will be in town?" He folded his napkin on the table, his lunch leaving no room for dessert or cake.

"It depends. Dan can use golf as an excuse, and Mom will forgive his absence."

"That's handy for him."

"Yeah, and Leanna usually comes home from college in Florida for the weekend."

He smiled. "It will be good for you to see your sister."

"I'm glad you'll have a chance to meet Leanna. She's lots of fun, and sporty like us, too."

He nodded toward the window. "Speaking of exercise, do you feel like a walk by the river?"

"A great idea. I'm too full to eat anything else."

"Me, too." He needed to walk off his lunch and walk off some stress and anxiety. He cared for Hannah and appreciated that she trusted him enough to share her family situation.

HANNAH SLIPPED her hand into Joel's, her fingers sliding through his as if they were a perfect fit. Her ponytail whipped around behind her as wind gusts shook branches on the trees in the park beside the river.

"Are you cold?" Concern filled his tone, and he slowed his pace.

"I'm good. The sun will keep me warm." It felt right to walk beside him, matching his stride, breathing in fresh air, and watching swans glide under the stone bridge.

They took the river path leading out of town. Pine and fir trees provided patches of shade from the heat in the afternoon sun.

She leaned into his shoulder, comfortable being close to him. "Can we take a break soon and rest on one of the bench seats?"

"Are you feeling tired?"

"Surprisingly no. Sometimes I just like to sit." She'd opened her heart to Joel at the Bellbird, sharing her personal pain regarding her strained relationship with Mom.

To be fair, all her siblings struggled to have a functional relationship with Mom. Becky's issues with Dad gave her common ground with Mom. Leanna argued with Mom all the time and was determined to never return and live in Trinity Lakes. Dan had checked out years ago, leaving Trinity Lakes in the rearview mirror.

Hannah sat beside Joel on a bench seat and shuffled closer, her leg resting beside his. He looped his arm around her shoulders, his touch light and reassuring. Without speaking any words, Joel seemed to understand she needed processing time. Digging up Mom memories had been an emotionally exhausting exercise.

Hannah had shied away from previous romantic relationship opportunities. She feared history would repeat itself, and she'd marry the wrong man. Her mother's bitterness, sown over the years, had dug roots in Hannah's heart and fed her fears and insecurities.

Her attraction and pull toward Joel was undeniable and unexpectedly comfortable. She'd prayed about Joel, and her fears regarding moving into a more serious relationship. She didn't want to let her emotions, combined with their mutual attraction, lead her on a merry path to heartbreak.

Joel shared her faith and their lives seemed to fit together. Was she falling in love with Joel? Could love be enough? Could they overcome other obstacles that would inevitably come their way?

He turned to face her. "What are you thinking?"

That was a loaded question. "I'm not sure you'd want to know."

"Try me." His gentle voice inspired her to open up and stamp out her fears.

She stared into his eyes. "We have something good going on."

He chuckled. "I agree, and I have a question."

"Okay." She held his steady gaze, his eyes soft and bright. "What's your question?"

"It's actually the question I should have asked before you stepped into the boat."

"Oh." She closed her eyes for a moment. "I kind of messed that up."

"No, it wasn't the right timing." He tucked a few strands of her hair behind her ear, his fingertip tracing the contour of her cheekbone. "Can I kiss you?"

She nodded. "Yes. Yes."

Her eyelids drifted closed, and he feathered kisses near her mouth, teasing her to welcome his kiss. She parted her lips, and he drew her closer, his touch tender and mind blowing and waking a response in her.

He pulled back, his breathing a little faster, his glittering eyes locking in her gaze and keeping their connection alive.

"Wow, Hannah. That was worth waiting for."

"Hmm." She cupped his face, her fingertips tracing over his jaw and five-o'clock shadow. "Can we do it again?"

He cracked a big grin. "I thought you'd never ask."

She ran her fingers through his hair and snuggled in his arms. She didn't want this day to end.

CHAPTER SEVEN

The next day, Joel lounged back in the passenger seat of his truck and stretched his legs. He was on his lunch break, and he was tired after a full morning of tiling work at a ranch out of town.

Hannah had sent him a text, and was waiting for his call. It was her day off, and she'd spent the morning on the country club golf course playing in a ladies tournament. He'd timed his lunch break to coincide with her break after playing eighteen holes.

He couldn't shift Hannah's amazing kisses from yesterday out of his mind. The depth of feelings their sweet kisses had ignited—feelings that were more intense than pure physical attraction—had thrown him off balance. Their honest and heartfelt conversations had laid the foundation for their close friendship to develop into something more.

Thankfully he had phone coverage where he'd parked on top of a hill beside a dirt road. The weather was overcast, and the temperature outdoors was pleasant. He'd lowered the truck windows to catch a wisp of a breeze. The dust had settled, and the distinctive cattle smells he associated with ranches were not wafting in through the windows.

He connected a call to Hannah and put his phone on speaker.

"Hey there, cowboy," she said.

He laughed. "You have the wrong guy. I can see cowboys riding in the distance."

"Where are you?"

"In my truck on a ranch, looking down into a valley full of cattle."

She chuckled. "Sounds exciting, and different to my lake views."

"Yeah, it's different all right." A couple of cowboys were mending a fence. A few others were riding with the cattle. Not a bad life for people who liked horses and working outdoors.

"What's for lunch?" she asked.

"Nothing you'd find exciting."

"You sure? My guess is Leah's chicken soup."

"Yes. Leah's soup and a Vegemite sandwich." He'd been surprised to discover he could buy Vegemite at a Trinity Lakes grocery store.

"I'm not visiting Australia if I have to eat Vegemite."

"Not all Aussies like Vegemite." He'd learned not to eat Vegemite anywhere near Hannah, but she was fun to tease.

"That's good to know. I've got ten minutes until I need to be in the restaurant."

He sipped his soup. "How was golf?"

"My game wasn't great." She paused. "I need to practice and play more before Dad visits."

"I'm guessing you won't be awarded any prizes at lunch." He took a bite of his Vegemite sandwich.

"Not today. The lunch special is Surf and Turf, which I'll call my consolation prize."

"Prawns or lobster?"

"I think it's shrimp. Walking eighteen holes has made me hungry."

No surprise there. Eighteen holes was around five miles. "When's your dad visiting?"

"Soon. I've got a few weeks to improve my game."

"You'll need to hit the driving range instead of the gym."

"I'll do both at the country club. Hey, you play golf, right?"

"I can hold my own." He'd been practicing with the guys at the public golf course, and at the short course beside the driving range.

"Would you like to play a round with me?"

"Sure, but you know you'll beat me, even taking into account handicaps."

"The score isn't important. It's my dad who'll judge my game, and I don't want to disappoint him."

"I can't imagine you ever disappointing him. The rowing club is doing well, and there's only so many hours in the day." Hannah put high expectations on herself, and she worked hard to meet those expectations.

"Which is why I must make the hours I do have count. What do you say? I'll buy lunch in the restaurant. If you're lucky, Surf and Turf will be on the menu."

"How can I say no?" He may not be able to impress Susannah Gilbertson, but he could try to make a good impression on Hannah's father by not embarrassing himself on the golf course.

"Okay, we can make the arrangements later. What time are you finishing today?"

"Around three-thirty." He hoped to leave earlier. "I'll be back tomorrow to finish the job."

"We can talk during your drive back to Trinity Lakes. How far out of town are you?"

Good question. He'd used the truck's GPS to find the ranch. "At least an hour and a half. Phone reception is less patchy once I reach the highway."

"Sounds good. Do you have dinner plans?"

"I'll buy takeout on my way home and have an early night. Do you have plans for tomorrow afternoon?"

"I'm visiting Becky, Grandma, and Mom in the afternoon at Mom's place. Mom canceled our family dinner because she's out of town for the weekend."

He swallowed another bite of his sandwich and sipped more soup. "Have you told your mother about us?"

"Not yet. That's the plan for tomorrow when I have Grandma and Becky with me. After I see Mom, we could have dinner."

"That works." Mum's name appeared on his screen. "Speaking of mothers, mine is trying to call me."

"Isn't it the middle of the night in Australia?"

He checked the time. "It's five in the morning in Sydney. I have to go. Mum never calls this early."

"I hope everything is okay, and I'll be praying."

"Thanks. I'll text you." He ended the call, and the phone rang before he had a chance to check his messages.

"Mum, what's wrong?"

"Joel, thank goodness you answered. What time is it there?"

"Thursday lunchtime. What's happening?"

"It's Bella. She's missing."

His stomach lurched, and he put his sandwich aside. "What do you mean by missing?"

"She pretended to go to bed, but instead snuck out her window before midnight."

His breath caught in his throat as he did the math. She'd been missing for at least five hours. "Did you hear her leave?"

"No, but I checked her room. I had a feeling something wasn't right."

"Is this the first time Bella has snuck out?" She was only fourteen. What was going on in her life?

"She's done it before, but never on a school night." Mum let out a sob, her voice muffled. "She's always back by five, when my alarm wakes me."

"Have you tried to call or message her?"

"She won't pick up or reply. She disabled the tracking app on her phone when we were arguing."

No wonder Mum was panicking. "What was the fight about?"

"Everything. She didn't like me asking why she was in the city at three in the morning."

He put aside his frustration at Bella's reckless behavior. It was more important to find her. "What about her friends? Have you contacted their parents?"

"That's the problem. Bella isn't hanging out with her friends from school. Her new boyfriend is from somewhere else. I don't know how they met, I don't know where he lives, and I don't know what they do together."

That last question was one Joel didn't want to contemplate in any detail. "I don't know how I can help, other than to pray."

"Did you speak to her last weekend?"

"Yes. She looked and sounded fine on our video call." His sister was secretive, and she hadn't let on that she was having problems at home or school or anywhere else.

"Joel, I'm trying not to panic, but Mike is offline. He's about to go into an important all-day meeting in Auckland that can't be postponed."

New Zealand's time zone was two hours ahead of Sydney. "You've spoken with him, right?"

"Before I called you. If Bella doesn't come home in time for school, we agreed that I'll tell the school she's missing, and go from there."

He ran his hand through his hair. Mum had complained about her hair turning gray. Bella had the whole family worried sick.

"Mum, I need to get back to work. I'm at a ranch and on a tight schedule."

"You're visiting a ranch with real cowboys." Her awestruck tone confirmed he'd temporarily distracted her from her worries.

"They're the real deal." What was the obsession with cowboys? Last weekend Bella had asked him a bunch of cowboy questions. They had cattlemen and women in Australia who wore Akubra hats and did the same job.

"Okay, honey. Please pray. I'll text when I have news."

"Love you, Mum. Take care of yourself, okay?"

"I'll try, but I miss having you near. Your year in the States can't end soon enough. Love you, too."

His throat tightened, and he swallowed the words that would reveal his growing relationship with Hannah. It wasn't the time, and Mum wouldn't be receptive to hearing about a potential threat to him returning home as planned.

"I'll look out for your message. Chat later." He ended the call and finished his soup. Oh boy, what was going on with Bella? How had things become this bad at home? He closed his eyes, praying she'd safely return home as soon as possible.

———

A WEEK LATER, Hannah led Joel to her downstairs storeroom filled with her father and brother's sporting equipment. She pulled a driver out of a golf bag. "This one might work. You're a similar height and build to Dan."

Joel stepped back into the hall, lining up the club on the wooden floor. "It feels like a better fit than the clubs I've borrowed from the college."

"The right clubs will improve your game." Hannah poked around in the golf bag. "It's a full set, too."

"I don't want to wreck your brother's clubs."

"They're sponsor gifts he's probably forgotten he owns."

"Okay. Thanks. I think these clubs will be good."

She checked her phone. "We should head over to the course, so we don't miss our tee time."

"I can drive. There's space in my truck for our clubs."

"That works for me." She collected her sweater and the pocket-sized purse she'd left on a stool at her kitchen island. Last week, Joel's family had been worried sick about Bella being missing. Their prayers for Bella's safety were answered, and she'd arrived home in time to get ready for school.

Joel balanced the golf bag on the floor beside him. "Does Dan have a house somewhere?"

"In Florida, near Leanna's college. Leanna often stays at Dan's place when he's away traveling."

"It's convenient they live close by."

She nodded. "Leanna doesn't like living in the dorm. Dan's house has a pool, a tennis court, and a good setup for outdoor entertaining."

Joel rolled his eyes. "That sounds like party central for Leanna and her college friends."

"Yeah, there's that. Speaking of sisters and partying, I'm glad Bella is behaving herself."

"For the time being." He crossed his arms over his chest. "She's home before curfew, and staying home all night, but who knows if it will last? If Bella had access to Dan's party house, she'd get herself into trouble."

"Thankfully Leanna is older and dedicated to her studies. It's the out-of-town trips to tennis tournaments that worry Mom." Now Leanna was away from Mom, she took full advantage of having freedom from scrutiny. Hannah prayed Leanna would find a nice group of church friends at college, rather than hanging around the jocks who played the college tennis circuit.

"I'm glad Leanna is enjoying college."

"Me, too. Becky hated being away for college, but Leanna

loves living in Florida." Hannah collected her golf clubs from her garage.

Joel hoisted their clubs into his truck. "Since Dan has his own place, why are you storing his stuff?"

A good question. She'd always had trouble saying no to her brother. "He often visits with a new set of clubs and sometimes leaves them here. He stops by when he's between tour events."

Joel shook his head. "Your brother's lifestyle sounds extravagant."

"Dan is actually a shy and private person, despite his public persona."

"He made an interesting career choice for someone who's shy."

"We grew up with Dad in the media spotlight. If you look at our social media accounts, you'll see they're business focused." Dad had taught them to be careful about what they shared online.

"That's wise, even if you're not in the limelight."

"Yeah, we have too many gossips in town, and we don't need to add online fuel to their fires."

Mom had already heard about her relationship with Joel before their Friday afternoon conversation with Grandma and Becky. Someone had seen Hannah and Joel sailing. Someone else had seen them at lunch at the Bellbird. But the biggest, creepiest gossip of all had seen them kissing by the river. Who else had been there? What kind of person spread that kind of gossip? Someone needed to get a life.

"Being anonymous is definitely an advantage for me living here," he said.

"For sure. Dan also has a house on the Oregon Coast. He can hide out there and avoid the media circus." The small Oregon town had a beautiful golf course located on cliffs beside the ocean.

"A smart plan." Joel drove the short distance to the country club parking lot.

A cloudless sky and morning sunshine would provide pleasant conditions on the course. Hannah had layered on sunscreen and made sure her hat was in her golf buggy bag.

Joel looked the part of a golfer, in his light blue polo top and beige slacks. She was used to seeing him wearing cargo pants or jeans. The country club had a strict dress code, and she wore a pale pink polo top tucked into her comfortable navy golf pants. Her hair was pulled back in a neat ponytail, and she'd cleaned her leather golf shoes.

"Have you played here before?" she asked.

He shook his head. "I've done maintenance work around the complex. It looks like a challenging course."

"It's championship level. Dad helped design the course, and he was instrumental in getting the old course up to world class standards."

He walked beside her along the path to the pro shop. "Did the redevelopment change the size of Gilbertson Pond?"

"I think it's now shorter and wider. They use excess river water for irrigation and to prevent flooding." The lush grass and wet greens were maintained by a team of groundskeepers who worked hard to keep the course in top condition.

"That makes sense. Are you ready to watch me embarrass myself?"

"You'll be fine."

"I'm an expert at slicing and hooking and overhitting the greens. Water hazards love collecting my golf balls."

She paused. "If you're concerned, I can give you some free coaching along the way. I don't mind. But only if you're inter-ested." She'd had a couple of golf dates turn sour when her date couldn't outperform her on the course and didn't appreciate her well-meaning feedback.

"That could be helpful. I'm not too proud to admit when I'm in over my head."

She grinned. "Teamwork is the best. If we work together and help each other, we'll get the best outcome."

He wrapped his arm around her shoulder and dropped a kiss on her welcoming lips. "We are good at teamwork."

Warmth flowed through her, her face heating from his casual display of affection. "I agree. Let's do this." Team Joel and Hannah would win the day and grow stronger together.

———

JOEL LINED up his opening drive shot on the eighteenth hole. Beads of sweat gathered on his forehead. The exertion from playing a few hours of golf had warmed his muscles and given him a cardio workout. Gilbertson Pond ran alongside the fairway, waiting for him to mishit his driver shot off the tee and devour his golf ball.

Hannah smiled. "You've got this. The fairway is a dogleg, and if you can hit high over the trees, you'll be within range of the green." Hannah took her own advice and used her driver to hit her ball exactly as she'd described.

"You do realize you make everything look easy, but it's actually really hard."

"The breeze is behind us, and it's not swirling above the trees. I believe in you."

He nodded, glad there was someone in the world who thought he could do it. At least a crow hadn't plucked any of his balls out of midair and stolen them. Those birds knew when to interfere and wreck the best shot he'd make all day.

He lined up his club and prayed for a clean swing. His driver made contact with the ball, and it flew high in the air, clearing the cluster of fir trees beside the fairway.

Hannah jumped up and down and gave him a brief hug. "I

knew you could do it." She grabbed her drink bottle from her golf bag. "Let's go see how well we did."

He pulled his golf bag behind him, drinking in her exuberant praise like a parched man stranded in the desert. His step was light now he didn't need to search for his ball in the trees or take a drop shot near the water ... two things he'd already had practice doing today.

"Wow, we did well." By some miracle he could only attribute to prayer and divine intervention, his golf ball was only thirty feet behind Hannah's.

"This hole is par four, and we're in a good position to birdie the hole."

Hannah selected an iron, and Joel followed her lead. He hit an okay second shot, the ball landing short of the green.

They walked ahead to Hannah's ball. Hannah hit her ball with perfect timing, and it rolled to a stop on the green within easy putting distance of the hole.

He clapped. "How did you do that?"

"Practice, practice, and more practice. I know the course and the capability of my clubs, which helps."

"I'll take your word for it."

"Now it's your turn to get your first birdie," she said.

"Honestly, I'd be happy with par." Or even one over on this hole. His handicap of twenty from last year, when he'd played weekly with a few mates and entered the golf club's Saturday tournaments, still put him miles behind Hannah's single digit handicap.

He chipped his third shot onto the green, the ball landing short of the hole, and rolling past the hole toward the far side of the green.

Hannah lined up her putting shot, on an uphill gradient, and gave the ball enough force to pop it straight into the hole. "A birdie for me."

He high-fived her. "Well done."

He tapped the ball with his putter, and it rolled six feet into the hole to make par. The only par he'd achieved on a par four or higher hole.

"Go you." She stretched on tiptoes, pressing a kiss on his cheek. "I'm proud of you."

Her smile melted his disappointment in his score. "My putting and short course game on the par three holes saved me from complete humiliation."

"This is a tough course, and you only lost three balls in the water."

"Three too many." He plucked his ball out of the hole and moved his clubs away from the edge of the green. The group behind were waiting to make their next shot. He'd lived in the sand bunkers, too, and was glad he'd practiced using a sand wedge to get out of trouble in the sand.

Hannah wheeled her golf bag behind her, looking like she had the energy to play another eighteen holes. "You'd be surprised how many balls they retrieve when they dredge the pond."

"Actually, I don't think I would be surprised. Not if enough members play as well as me."

She laughed. "The balls are repurposed for the practice range."

"Do you use the range often?"

"I try to." She walked beside Joel toward the club and the restaurant on the lower level overlooking Gilbertson Pond. "Dad taught us how to play on the driving range. I can still hear his voice, telling me to bend my knees, straighten my back, adjust my grip. Years of training has drilled his coaching into my head."

"And you never considered following in his footsteps, like Dan?"

She shook her head. "No way. I prefer the solitude of rowing and kayaking. Golf is too full-on and too big a commitment."

"The pro tour is year-round."

"Yeah, and the thought of living out of a suitcase isn't appealing. I'm happy with my life here."

"That's fair." He understood Hannah's attachment to Trinity Lakes, and the small-town lifestyle it offered.

Hannah left her golf clubs in a shaded area near the outdoor restaurant seating. "I've booked a table under the awning to make the most of the beautiful weather."

He nodded. "A good idea. I'm ready to enjoy being outdoors and out of the sun."

She studied his tanned forearms. "You're not sunburned."

"I'm fine." He'd layered on the sunscreen, used to protecting his skin from the harsh Australian sunshine.

She glanced at the specials blackboard next to the door. "You're in luck. Surf and Turf is on the menu."

He reached for her hands and drew her close. "Thank you for today. Let's celebrate me surviving the course with Surf and Turf."

She grinned. "Sounds good to me."

He led Hannah indoors, looking forward to a leisurely lunch with the woman who'd made him believe he had a second chance at finding love.

———

HANNAH DABBED a white linen napkin on the corner of her mouth and discreetly checked the time on her sports watch. Thirty minutes until she could make her excuses and escape Mom's family dinner. Mom had made a last-minute summons, requesting Hannah bring Joel to dinner tonight.

Mom was seated at the head of her long table in the formal dining room, and the silverware was nowhere in sight. Hannah sat between Mom and Joel, with Becky and Grandma opposite. So far Mom had behaved, and dinner had run smoothly. Becky had helped Grandma clear their entree plates, and they were in the kitchen organizing apple pie for dessert.

Mom sipped her water. "Joel, tell me, why are you staying in a dorm?"

Joel paused, glass halfway to his mouth. He took his time sipping his water before answering. "It didn't make sense to set up a rental in town when I'd be traveling for part of the year."

"You're only here temporarily, right?" Mom lifted her chin and looked down her nose, condescension lacing her fake-sweet tone. "Does Hannah know your plans?"

"Mom, it's fine." Hannah turned to Joel, her eyes communicating it was game on. How could she shut down this conversation? "Of course Joel wants to travel and see our beautiful country."

He nodded, his expression polite and smile intact. "I'm hoping to visit Canada, too."

"That's a busy itinerary," Mom said. "How many months will you be away from Trinity Lakes?"

"I'm not sure." He held Mom's gaze, playing the cat and mouse game Hannah knew all too well. "I'll be traveling during summer."

"Doesn't that sound fun, Mom? I wish I could take a summer off for a vacation."

"Yes, dear, but you hold a responsible job with people who rely on you." Mom turned back to Joel, her smile failing to mask her superiority. "I hear you do some kind of tiling work."

He nodded. "I have a trade qualification."

"Did you attend college, or drop out?"

"Mom, really? What's with the twenty questions?"

Mom shrugged off Hannah's question, as if it wasn't appropriate to query her motives. "I'm interested in learning more about Joel, since he's your new friend."

New friend. Hannah couldn't dodge the shooting arrow this time, and it plunged into the heart of her hopes and dreams.

Mom didn't like Joel, and she'd waited until it was just the three of them to spread her venom cloaked in nice words.

He cleared his throat. "I chose not to attend university."

Mom's eyes widened, as if not attending university was unthinkable. "I'm sure your parents were disappointed you chose a trade instead of a proper education."

Hannah's hand flew to her mouth. No. No. No. Did Mom really say that?

Joel sat straighter in his chair, his mouth set in a firm line. It seemed like Mom's words had bounced off him and landed in the table centerpiece display of fragrant roses. "My parents are happy to let me make my own decisions, and they support my choices."

Bang. Mom's face flinched, as if the vase of roses had been poured over her head. "Where is our apple pie? Are they growing the apples in the kitchen?"

Becky walked into the dining room, pie in hand. "Who grows apples in their kitchen?"

Mom shook her head. "It's nothing, dear. Just waiting for dessert."

Grandma appeared, carrying a tray that included clotted cream and ice cream. "Are we ready for dessert?"

"Yes," Hannah said. "We need to leave as soon as we finish eating. Early start tomorrow." Round one to Joel. Mom always changed the conversation topic when she was stumped for a suitable response. Of course, Mom now acted as if the conversation with Joel had never happened. Hannah would let her think she'd won and that she'd scared Joel away. Dessert couldn't finish soon enough.

CHAPTER EIGHT

Joel pulled out of the parking lot near Cohen's, his truck loaded with hardware supplies for Hannah's bathroom. She'd noticed a grout issue in her en suite shower, and he'd offered to fix it this morning.

His boss had employed another tiler, a young guy with a family to support who was new to town. Joel's workload had lessened, and the cut in overtime hours provided more time for other things, including maintenance work at the Bible college. Hannah had replied to his message, letting him know she was gardening in her backyard with Gracie.

He turned onto Hannah's street. Spring flowers bloomed in the front yards of well-maintained houses with sweeping views over Trinity Lakes and the mountains. He reversed into Hannah's drive, parking in front of the garage where Hannah kept her SUV.

Becky used the double-length carport beside the garage that opened into the backyard, providing space to store her compact coffee cart trailer.

Joel unloaded his truck and carried supplies around to Hannah's back door. The tradies' entrance, as it was known in

Australia, was closest to the internal flight of stairs to the upper level.

"Joel!" Gracie walked toward him, dirt stains on her track pant knees and gardening gloves covering her hands.

He greeted her and searched the yard. "Is Hannah around?"

"She's inside, making coffee with Becky's coffee beans."

"Coffee sounds good." He'd woken late and hadn't had time to detour for a caffeine fix. He could take or leave coffee, except if it was Becky's brew. He suspected she used the same supplier as the Bellbird.

Gracie removed her gloves. "Follow me. I believe there are cinnamon rolls to go along with coffee."

Joel chuckled. "How can I say no to cinnamon rolls?"

"You can't." Gracie stopped by the laundry inside the back door and washed her hands.

He followed her, cleaning up and wiping his hands dry on a hand towel. "How am I supposed to get any work done if my day starts with a coffee break and cinnamon rolls?"

"It's called energy food, young man. I started gardening at seven-thirty, before the sun was hot. I'm counting this as breakfast."

"That works. Hannah's fortunate to have your help in the garden."

"It keeps me young and gives me an excuse to leave the house early." She shook her head, gray curls bouncing around her face. "I'm sorry about my daughter. Susannah is difficult to manage, and I told her she's being unfair."

He nodded. Susannah had initially been pleasant during dinner, and she'd lured Joel into a false sense of security. Her demeaning behavior and verbal insults before dessert had upset Hannah, and Joel was in no rush for a repeat performance. "I appreciate yours and Becky's support."

"We're both in your corner. Susannah is stubborn, and she struggles to be happy for other people. It's not personal."

"That's what Hannah keeps saying." How could he not take it personally? Susannah had waited until Gracie and Becky were out of the room, and made sure Joel got the message that he wasn't good enough for Hannah.

"It really isn't, Joel. My dear late husband was a surgeon who provided well for us financially. He spoiled our only child, and she's grown up with an entrenched entitlement mentality."

A polite way of saying Susannah was an obnoxious snob. "I don't have a college education, but I'm not exactly short of money." His stepfather's wealth would rival Hannah's father, but he'd keep that information to himself.

"Susannah is narrow-minded and won't listen to reason. She upset Hannah, but she refuses to admit she's wrong because she always thinks she's right."

Joel blew out a long breath, choosing his words carefully. "I know she's your daughter, and families are complicated, but I'm not prepared to put up with Susannah's behavior."

Gracie nodded. "I understand, and I wish I had the power to make my daughter see sense. Have you spoken with Hannah and told her what you've told me?"

He rubbed his hand over his jaw. "We agreed I'll skip the weekly dinners unless Susannah does something to suggest she'll change her attitude. I'll go to the birthday and Mother's Day celebration." A larger and less intense gathering, where Susannah was unlikely to embarrass herself by making a scene.

Gracie gave him a small smile. "That sounds like a good compromise."

"We're trying to prevent Susannah from causing problems between me and Hannah." A challenge that currently seemed insurmountable.

"I'm truly sorry Susannah is behaving this way. She attends church services every Sunday morning, but it doesn't seem to make a difference."

"It's hard, but we'll try to ignore her negativity." Becky had been blunt in sharing her thoughts with Joel on what Becky described as her mother's appalling and unchristian behavior.

"I'm glad to hear this," Gracie said.

Joel followed Gracie into Hannah's spacious kitchen and dining area overlooking the deck.

"Hey." Hannah walked into his hug and dropped a kiss on his lips. "You're right on time. Coffee and cinnamon rolls are ready to serve."

"Sounds good." Joel pulled out a chair at the table, glad the family dinner fiasco hadn't disrupted his relationship with Hannah. The aroma of warm cinnamon rolls mingling with coffee teased his taste buds.

Hannah sat opposite and pushed down on the French press. "Becky has convinced me that the old-fashioned French press is the best alternative to her espresso machine."

Gracie clasped her hands together. "Of course it is. I don't know why people switched to using those pods or instant coffee."

"Convenience." Hannah poured coffee into three mugs. A small jug of cream, a bowl of sugar, teaspoons, and napkins, were in the middle of the table.

"My mother can ruin plunger coffee," Joel said.

Hannah's eyebrows shot up. "Plunger coffee. What is that?"

Gracie chuckled. "The French press. I've been researching Aussie expressions, and I still don't get why you say you eat bangers and mash."

"It's complicated." Joel grinned. "I think you'll find the Brits came up with the bangers and mash saying to describe English pub food." Beef sausages and mashed potato were part of his diet growing up in Australia.

"Oh." Hannah's gaze fixed on her grandma. "Joel can make you a Vegemite sandwich, and then you'll know more than you ever wanted about Aussie food."

Gracie raised her hands. "I wasn't born yesterday, and I'm not falling for the Vegemite party trick."

He laughed. "Have you tried Vegemite? It's not as bad as people make out."

"I'm allergic." Gracie scrunched her nose. "I can't have too much yeast." She selected a cinnamon roll and spooned butter on top. "Of course, cinnamon rolls are fine with their small amount of yeast."

"Of course." Hannah nodded. "Becky's baking is going to send me to the gym every day."

"You and me, both." He stirred cream into his coffee, adding more calories.

Gracie turned to Hannah. "Your mother is being stubborn and won't listen to me."

"It's okay. She does have our best interests at heart," Hannah said.

Gracie harrumphed and sliced open her roll. "Sometimes there isn't a bright side or a glass half full. I fear my daughter won't be happy with any of the people my grandchildren choose to date."

"But Grandma, when she gets to know Joel, she'll have to come around to my point of view."

Gracie's steady gaze shifted between Hannah and Joel. "I'm sorry to burst your bubble, my dear, but you'll both need to accept she may never be happy. It's also not your job to make her happy."

He nodded. Gracie spoke common sense, as always. He appreciated her candid and supportive remarks.

Hannah sipped her coffee. "Why can't everyone just get along?"

"Because we live in a broken world," Gracie said. "Which is why we all need Jesus."

Hannah dipped her head forward and kept her thoughts to

herself. Her attention was focused on spreading butter over her cinnamon roll and dodging Joel's gaze.

Joel ate his cinnamon roll, chewing over their conversation. They couldn't control whether or not Susannah chose to support their relationship. All they could do was make the best of the present circumstances and pray for wisdom regarding future decisions.

Gracie finished her last bite of cinnamon roll. "That was a good breakfast. Joel, I'll be on the sideline at the AFL game on Saturday, cheering you on."

Joel smiled. "I appreciate your support." He appreciated Gracie claiming him as one of her own. It felt good to belong and have people in his corner.

Gracie rose, pushing back her chair. "I best go back outside and finish weeding."

"Thanks, Grandma." Hannah's smile was weak, her face revealing her conflicting emotions. "You know I'll always love you, even when you tell me hard facts."

"I know, honey. I do my best to help all my grandchildren cope with my daughter's problems."

Gracie was right. These problems belonged to Hannah's mother, and it wasn't their emotional baggage to carry or fix. He prayed Hannah could see the truth behind her mother's words and actions, and make wise decisions. Their future may depend on it.

———

HANNAH FINISHED FOLDING her laundry and headed upstairs to her bedroom. Becky's car had pulled up on the drive, and she'd be busy cleaning up her coffee cart and getting it organized for tomorrow.

Joel was in her en suite bathroom, chipping away at something. She stored her clothes in her walk-in wardrobe and walked over to the en suite entrance.

"How's the shower going?" she asked.

"As expected." Joel looked up in Hannah's direction. He shuffled backwards and sat on the folded towel he'd placed on the tiled floor outside the shower cubicle. "You were right about the grout not being waterproof."

"I'm glad you have time to fix it."

His smile lit up his face. "You know I'll always make time to help you."

His words warmed her heart and softened the rough edges created by her mother's hostility. "I appreciate you. Are you doing a full reseal?"

"I sure am, and it may be a good idea to think about resealing all your bathroom showers."

"Okay. We can check our schedules and book some dates. Thursdays are probably best."

"No worries." He stood, lifting his muscular arms above his head to stretch out his back muscles.

She looked away. It was time to think about something other than Joel looking like he belonged in her bathroom.

She pressed her lips together, knowing she couldn't avoid the awkward conversation topic known as her mother.

"Joel, I'm sorry Grandma was a bit full-on earlier." When Grandma had a bee in her bonnet, she didn't stop buzzing until everyone had heard her issues and listened to her perspective.

Joel crossed his arms over his chest. "You know she's right, don't you?"

"My mother is right." She shook her head. "You can't be serious?"

"No, Hannah. Gracie is right about your mother."

She let out a soft sigh. "It's really hard, Joel. Hard to accept Mom can't be happy that I'm happy."

"We'll keep praying and hoping for a miracle. In the meantime, we have to deal with the facts. We can choose how we respond."

"Yeah. I wish our circumstances were different."

"Hey." He stepped closer, tipping up her chin until she met his gaze. "It honestly could be a lot worse. You said your dad is happy for us, and I'll get to meet him soon."

"True. Dad has always been my rock. He's solid and dependable and I can trust him."

"Which is good, right?" He stepped away and surveyed her shower. "I should be done in an hour. We can have lunch and do something fun this afternoon."

"I need some fun today." Something to distract her from the very real problems in her family. "I'll think on some ideas that will work at short notice."

"That's my girl." He dropped a kiss on her forehead. "I'll get back to work and we can make plans soon."

"Sounds good." Hannah headed downstairs and entered her kitchen. Becky stood over the sink, washing dishes, her long gloves covering forearms that were almost elbow deep in sudsy water.

"How's the bathroom going?" Becky asked.

"Joel should be done in an hour." She sat on a tall stool at the kitchen island. "What am I going to do about Mom?

"Nothing. It's her problem, not yours or mine. Anyway, I have bigger issues to worry about."

"Oh, what's happened? Has something gone wrong with the coffee cart?"

"No, it's fine. My problem is Dad." Becky ramped up her dish scrubbing, soap suds sloshing onto the island around the sink. "I'm so angry I could scream."

"Please don't. Joel will think someone is being murdered."

"Ha ha but I'm serious. Dad is so controlling, and he's gone too far this time."

Hannah sucked in a deep breath, slowly counting to five.

She'd clear her mind of angry thoughts about Mom, hear Becky out, and resist the temptation to defend Dad. "What's happened?"

Becky threw her hands in the air, soap suds flying everywhere. "I put together a business plan to expand my operations for the coffee cart."

"Go you! That's a step in the right direction." She shifted her stool further away from the sink and flying soap suds, resisting the temptation to wipe the island dry.

"You'd think so, right?" Her sister placed her palms flat on the island, bouncing on her toes. "I've gone through the accounts, like you suggested, and worked out my margins."

"You're running at a profit." Never mind the financials. Becky was running on too much caffeine, judging by her inability to stand still.

"I am, and my stock levels have evened out. The website ordering, combined with a few promotions I've been doing with other businesses in town, has set me up in a good position for summer."

"I'm happy for you. You've finished paying off the cart costs, too."

Her sister nodded and plunged her hands back in the sink. "I put together a plan to gradually expand my opening hours on weekends, and during summer and school breaks. That means I could cut back my hours at the bakery, and the high schoolers can cover my bakery shifts."

"It's a long day of work for you, when you add in the bakery shifts."

Becky slowed down and sighed, looking like she'd run out of steam. "I'm tired of feeling like I'm working all the time. If you weren't letting me live here for cheap, I wouldn't be able to afford the business."

"I'm proud of you." Hannah gave her sister an encouraging smile. "Everything you've achieved has happened because you work hard and invest additional income from the bakery job in your business."

Becky added cake sliders and serving tongs to the dishwasher. "My costs keep going up, the prices of coffee beans and other expenses rise, and I can't necessarily cover all the rising costs by increasing my prices."

"It's a tricky balance, working out how much your customers are willing to pay, and knowing you have competitors nearby who can easily service your customers."

"I'm so glad you did a business degree and understand my dilemma. I need to spend money to make money, and I need capital to invest in an expansion."

"Oh, I can see where this is going." Dad had locked Becky's trust fund up tight after she quit college. "Did you approach Dad and he said no?"

"He didn't just say no. He's not prepared to release any money from my trust fund unless I can convince him my current business plan won't fail."

"Have you shown him the data, and sent him a copy of your accounts?" Becky had sacrificed a lot to invest all her time and savings into her business.

"Of course I have." Becky rinsed the last platter, placed it on the drainer, and let the water flow out of the sink. "He's insisting on seeing my business in action when he next visits by looking over my shoulder and checking up on me. He doesn't trust me, Hannah."

"I wouldn't go that far. I'm not sure how much money you've asked him to release, but it's true that most small businesses fail within the first few years."

Becky shot her an angry look. "You're taking his side! Really?"

"No, Becky. I'm expressing an opinion that Dad is looking out for your best interests."

"How does that work exactly?" She pulled off her rubber

gloves, dumping them beside the sink. "Since I quit college, I haven't asked for or received any money from my trust fund. Everything I've achieved is my own doing."

Hannah tucked loose strands of hair back behind her ears. "Dad will want to see for himself that your business has the potential to grow and succeed if more funds are invested."

Becky placed her hands on her hips. "Did he do this to you at the rowing club, before your twenty-fifth birthday?"

"I didn't take the reins fully until after my birthday. I spent a lot of time learning the ropes, so I understood all aspects of the business, including how to manage and negotiate the landlord arrangements. I still seek advice from Dad. I have my college degree—"

"And that's the difference. I'm the college dropout who won't amount to anything."

She shook her head. "That's so not true. It's not what Dad thinks, either."

"He's still angry I quit college and wasted his money."

"You could repay him, if it's an issue ..." Did they need to revisit the college issue today? She'd thought Dad and Becky had negotiated a truce and started to understand each other's perspective.

"Well, I offered, and he refused. He said I need to be responsible and follow through on my commitments."

Ditto. Not that she'd speak those words aloud. "You've got to concede that's a fair point. Dad is an astute businessman, and he started out dirt poor. Unlike Mom, he does understand how the other half live."

"Don't start me on Mom, and how snobby she's being. Dad's insisting on being my shadow and watching me work. It's so frustrating ..."

"But it's also an opportunity. If you can impress him with your growth potential, he may authorize your trust fund to invest more money than you requested."

Becky leaned forward on her elbows, choosing a dry section of the kitchen island. "Do you seriously think Dad would do that?"

"You won't know unless you give him a chance. We'll play golf with him, and that's when he talks business. You know the drill."

"Yeah, the boys club on the golf course and hanging around the country club really isn't my scene."

She tapped her foot on the floor. Becky needed to calm down and listen. "Okay. Breathe. Take a step back. Think like a savvy businesswoman. Treat him the way you'd treat a potential investor who wanted to learn the true value of your business. Put aside the emotions."

Becky rolled her eyes. "You know that's easier said than done."

They were making progress. "If I can ignore and deflect Mom's unnecessary negative commentary on Joel, you can put aside your bias and give Dad a chance. See him as a business partner who wants to help you."

"That's if he does want to help me. Maybe he wants to shut me down."

"Oh Becky." She squeezed her lips together. Could her sister take a moment and see the situation from Dad's perspective? "I'll pray you'll have an open mind and impress Dad with your hard work and dedication."

"Thank you. Prayers are always helpful."

"What's the worst thing that can happen? He says no, and you look for an alternative investor."

Becky gave her a hug. "You're good at talking me off the ledge."

"That's what big sisters are for. Also, I need your help with Mom."

"We'll survive Mother's Day, and you'll have Leanna home to distract Mom."

She lifted a brow. "What's Mom's issue with Leanna this time?"

"Take your pick. Dan let it slip that Leanna was having her college friends staying over at his house when he's away."

"Is this a problem for Dan?"

"Not anymore. He's negotiated house rules with Leanna that Mom thinks aren't strict enough."

"Oh boy." Her brother's lifestyle was too free and easy for Mom's liking. He was twenty-eight years old and hadn't lived under Mom's roof for over a decade. Leanna would soon turn twenty-one, and she had a good head on her shoulders.

"The Leanna distraction should work in your favor. We'll work together with Grandma to stop Mom from causing any more trouble."

"Thank you. I'll see what I can learn from Dad regarding your business and put in a good word for you." Becky deserved Dad's support. Hannah prayed Dad would see the potential in Becky's business and show Becky he believed in her.

THE FOLLOWING MONDAY, Hannah shut down her office computer at the rowing club and stretched her arms above her head. Tabby was taking care of the tourist groups who'd hired kayaks for the afternoon.

Hannah stood, flexing her fingers. The accounts were now up to date, and the outstanding invoices paid. Joel would be arriving soon, and they'd have afternoon tea before hitting the water in a two-person rowing boat.

Unless Joel suggested they do a warm-up run first. She'd cycled to work, but he probably wouldn't have his bike in his truck. He'd been working all day, with no time to leave the jobsite and visit during his lunch break.

Hannah left her office and walked over to the kitchen area in the clubhouse. Grandma stood next to the cookie jar, the electric kettle bubbling away.

Tabby walked indoors, a relaxed smile on her face. "The groups are on the water, and I'm stopping for a tea break."

"Thanks, Tabby. I think I'll join you."

"When's Joel arriving?" Grandma asked.

"In ten or fifteen minutes, maybe longer. He's looking forward to afternoon tea."

Grandma grinned. "I heard there's a black tea blend called Australian Afternoon Tea. I wonder if that's what Aussies drink in the afternoon."

Tabby chuckled. "You'll have to ask Joel when he arrives."

"The Aussies enjoyed their football game on Saturday," Grandma said. "All that kicking and running up and down the field."

Tabby nodded. "It was fun to watch. Hannah, would you like me to pour your tea, or will you wait for Joel?"

"I'll wait, thanks." One cup of tea was all she needed.

Grandma used a small pair of tongs to retrieve a triple chocolate chip cookie from near the bottom of the jar. "Someone else must like my favorite cookies."

"There's plenty for everyone." Hannah declined a cookie, not wanting to eat before she trained. "Tabby, is there anything I need to know?"

Tabby shook her head. "We got a last-minute booking for a group of schoolkids to row after school. They're regulars, and we have the equipment available."

"Good, good." Hannah sat at the table opposite Grandma. "Why are you really visiting this afternoon?"

"I'm sick of listening to your mother complaining about Leanna, and about Dan not being strict enough with her."

Hannah sighed. "Mom won't let it go."

Tabby placed her mug of hot tea on the table and sat beside Hannah. "Oh, I know what I forgot to tell you."

"Please tell me it has nothing to do with my mother."

"No, it's about Kyla." Tabby sipped her tea. "She's engaged to Caleb."

Hannah lifted her eyebrows. "Really? When did that happen?"

Tabby shrugged. "I'm not sure. Kyla was showing off her engagement ring at the AFL game."

Grandma cleared her throat. "There is a story—"

"No." Hannah placed her hands over her ears. "I don't want to hear any gossip. Why can't people be happy for them?"

Tabby pursed her lips. "I hate to say this Hannah, but I feel a bit sorry for Caleb. I don't know if he realizes what he's getting into with Kyla."

"Tabby." She let out an exasperated breath. "I know you're not a fan of Kyla's, but she seems like she'd be happy as a pastor's wife."

Grandma nodded. "And that's what people are talking about. Kyla's ambitions for her future husband."

Hannah shook her head. "Not you too, Grandma. Why don't you like Kyla?"

Grandma munched on her cookie and sipped her tea. "Tabby is right. Kyla is a complex person."

"What do you mean?" Hannah asked.

"My sweet girl, I know you want to see the best in everyone, even when there's little good to be found. Sometimes we miss the obvious things in front of our noses because we don't want to see them."

"Huh?" Hannah twisted her hands together in her lap. "Would you like to repeat that in English?"

Tabby snickered. "I want to adopt your grandma."

Grandma patted Tabby's hand. "I love you too, honey." She turned to Hannah. "It's admirable to want to see the best in people. The truth is they may fail to meet your expectations because you won't acknowledge the existence of their faults."

"You're talking about Mom?" Hannah asked.

"I'm talking about people in general. I can see Kyla's true character, and Caleb may not have an easy time being married to her. But that's his life and his choice."

"That's fair." She looked up and met Tabby's gaze. "I'm sorry I brush off your issues with Kyla."

"Apology accepted." Tabby continued sipping her tea. "You don't see Kyla's other side because she's always trying to flatter and impress you. Whereas I'm a nobody."

"No Tabby, please don't say that. You're a wonderful and gifted person, and my best friend."

Grandma polished off her cookie. "We can all agree Tabby's amazing, and Kyla doesn't care to see it. But that's Kyla's loss, not something to dwell on."

"Well said." Tabby's phone beeped. She picked up her phone, her attention riveted to the screen. "I've got more important things to worry about than Kyla."

Grandma stood and placed her hand on Tabby's shoulder. "Don't you give that girl another thought. Her opinion of you doesn't matter."

Tabby smiled. "Thanks, Grandma Gracie."

Hannah leaned back in her seat and watched Grandma walk outside. "One day I hope to be even half as smart as Grandma."

"Yeah, she's awesome. Can we talk about something important?"

"Sure, what's up?"

"I just got a text from Dad. It's about the expert we hired to investigate the zoning of the floodplain." Tabby opened her phone and scrolled down the screen.

"You have an answer." Hannah had postponed doing her own research. It was on her to-do list.

Tabby nodded slowly, her expressive eyes revealing her conflicted feelings. "The expert couldn't find a single reason to explain why our land was zoned as a floodplain."

Her jaw fell slack. "There must be a reason, or it wouldn't have happened."

Tabby shook her head. "I'm sorry, Hannah. Our guy was thorough, and he investigated every possible angle. He can't explain why the land was designated a floodplain."

She closed her eyes, letting Tabby's words sink in. Someone must know something. Someone must have done something to change the zoning.

She opened her eyes. "I'll look into it, and we'll find out what happened."

"It's a mystery. Gran might have known, but..." Tabby took a deep breath, as though she was fighting to hold back tears.

"Leave it with me. I'll do some research and see what I can dig up." She glanced at the clock. "Joel is due any minute. Can you let him know I'll be in my office, and I won't be long?"

"Sure." Tabby stood. "I'll get back to work on my job list."

"Thank you." Hannah strode toward her office, her steps firm and unyielding. She knew who to call, and she'd pay top dollar to get a report completed as fast as possible. The sooner she refuted or confirmed the findings of Tabby's expert, the sooner she could learn what had gone down in Trinity Lakes over twenty years ago.

CHAPTER NINE

A week later, Hannah reclined in a deck chair on her back deck, her lower legs and bare feet warming in the morning sun. Book club was on next week, and she wanted to be organized and finish reading their May selection, Dear Henry, Love Edith by Becca Kinzer. She loved romcoms, and loved the story, but her mind was preoccupied.

She closed the reading app on her tablet and opened her email program. Her guy, Robert, had sent through his report on the flood zoning an hour ago, and she'd read every word in the report three times.

Robert's report backed up the findings from Tabby's expert. There was no paper trail and no evidence available to support the decision to change the zoning to a floodplain.

Hannah downed the dregs of her lukewarm coffee. It didn't make sense. There had to be a reason for the zoning change.

She picked up her phone and connected a call to Robert. He answered within seconds.

"Hey, Hannah, did you get my email?"

"Yes, Robert, and thanks for getting the job done quickly."

"You're welcome. Do you have any questions?"

"I have a few. Is it unusual for a zoning change to not have a paper or electronic trail?"

"Not necessarily. We're going back over twenty years, and smaller towns tend to do things differently to Spokane or Olympia."

"I get that, but does it seem odd that a zoning change that significantly altered the land values doesn't have any supporting documentation on file."

Robert paused. "I've heard about situations like this before."

"Please tell me more. What did those situations have in common?"

"This is strictly off the record, and I'd never put this in writing."

"Sure. I really want to learn the truth."

"And that's the problem."

"Huh? I'm not following."

"Someone, or a group of someone's, may have put in a lot of effort to suppress the reasons for the zoning change."

She gasped. "No. Are you saying it's possible that something underhanded took place?"

"I'm not saying anything for certain. But anything is possible."

Hannah's mind started ticking over, her love for mystery novels providing a dozen possible scenarios involving bribery, corruption, and foul play. "Hypothetically speaking, if I wanted to dig further, what are my options?"

"You could hire a private investigator. That would be expensive, and you'd have difficulty keeping your search anonymous in a small town where everyone knows everyone's business."

Except for when they didn't know each other's business. Someone in town at the time must have known something. "I don't think a private investigator is a viable option."

"You could ask your father and see what he remembers. Wasn't he mayor around that time?"

"Yeah, that's a possibility." She hadn't thought to check the dates to see if they matched.

"The zoning decision included your father's land. If the town had followed correct processes, and your father had owned the land prior to the zoning change, he would have been notified."

"That makes sense. Thank you for your time."

"You're welcome, and I hope you find your answers."

"Me, too." She ended the call, her mind replaying conversations with Dad.

Dad had told her about the flood zoning when she'd finished college and returned to Trinity Lakes to work at the rowing club. He'd never mentioned any problems with the zoning decision. It didn't seem to bother him that the bulk of his waterfront land, the land he'd transferred to her trust fund, was blocked from being developed.

Hannah closed her eyes, her memories coming thick and fast. It didn't add up. Something didn't feel right.

Dad was arriving in Trinity Lakes in two days to visit with her. She'd find an opportunity to bring up the subject and discover what he knew about the process behind the flood zoning decision. She'd speak to Dad before updating Tabby. One way or another, she'd uncover the truth and solve the mystery.

———

ON SATURDAY AFTERNOON, Joel drove past Hannah's home on his way to the country club. He'd spent the morning playing soccer with the guys, and they'd made burgers for lunch. He'd volunteered to man the grill before he knew Hannah's father would be in town.

Hannah had arranged, at the last minute, to take the day off work. She'd organized an early lunch with her father and Becky, before hitting the golf course to play eighteen holes.

Becky wanted to talk business with their father during the golf round, so it wasn't a problem that Joel had a prior commitment.

Joel was booked in to play nine holes with Hannah and her father tomorrow afternoon. Nine holes was a less daunting prospect than eighteen. Nine fewer opportunities to mess up his shots and double or triple bogey the holes.

Joel parked his truck and walked along the path leading to the downstairs restaurant with outdoor seating. He'd changed into a polo top, ensuring he met the posh country club dress code requirements.

Joel opened a text from Hannah.

We're at hole 17. Meet you at the restaurant.

He replied with a smile and a heart, ordered a Coke, and chose an outdoor table in the shade with a clear view of the eighteenth hole.

Joel wiped sweaty palms on a napkin and sipped his drink. He could blame the hot afternoon weather for his red-tinged skin, but his somersaulting stomach gave away the truth. He was nervous about meeting Hannah's father. Her famous father, at least in golfing circles.

Joel's golfing mates in Australia had watched Hannah's father play golf on television. They knew her brother, too, and followed Dan's career.

Joel's sporting credentials consisted of two international junior rowing meets, one in England and one in New Zealand. Kicking three goals in the recent AFL game and one goal in soccer today couldn't compete with the achievements of Hannah's father or brother.

A group finished up at the eighteenth hole, the players not having any luck with their putting. He could relate and empathize with their frustration. He spotted Hannah, Becky, and their dad walking along the fairway.

Becky lined up a shot from the bend in the dogleg on the

fairway. The ball flew low in the air and landed short of the green.

Hannah walked further along the fairway and moved into position to take her next shot. It looked like her drive shot off the tee had cleared the cluster of trees, landing in a similar spot to the last time they'd played. Her next shot seemed effortless, landing a foot from the hole, and rolling a few feet away. He smiled, proud of her golfing abilities.

The group continued along the fairway, stopping for their dad to make his next shot. Wayne Gilbertson timed the ball beautifully, and it landed on the green and rolled into the hole.

Joel clapped, admiring the skill of a master player who'd likely scored an eagle on the eighteenth hole. Two under par, on a par four hole, was a result Joel could only dream about unless he fluked two excellent shots in a row.

Becky's next shot landed on the green, close to the hole. Hannah putted her ball into the hole, and high-fived her sister in what Joel assumed was a birdie celebration. Becky took two putts to land her ball in the hole.

Becky led the group to the outdoor seating and made a beeline for Joel's table. "Hey Joel, did you watch me mess up the final hole?"

Joel grinned. "You play better than I do."

"But not as good as Dad or my siblings." She pulled out a chair and collapsed into the seat.

"You win when it's important—with great coffee."

"If you keep up the compliments, your next coffee will be on the house."

"That works for me." Joel switched his attention to Hannah and her father, who had reached his table.

Hannah dropped a kiss on his lips and whispered in his ear. "You've got this. Dad won't bite."

Hannah made the introductions, and Joel shook her father's hand, his grip firm.

Wayne smiled. "It's good to finally meet you, Joel. My Hannah can't stop talking about you."

"Dad." Hannah swatted her father with her hat. "You're so embarrassing."

Wayne hugged Hannah's shoulders. "I'm happy you're happy. Anyway, who'd like a drink?"

"I'll get the drinks." Becky stood. "Joel, would you like a refill?"

"I'm good, thanks." He was glad Hannah had slipped into the seat beside him.

"Dad, Hannah, your usual?"

Hannah nodded. "Please."

"Thanks, Becky." Wayne sat opposite Joel, his gaze warm and assessing.

Joel held Wayne's gaze. "I was impressed by what looked like an eagle."

"Yes, and well done on making the connection. The breeze stilled at the right time, and Hannah got her birdie."

"My score today was good." Hannah's relief was evident in her bright eyes.

"Congratulations to you both."

Hannah's father relaxed back into his seat, his attention drawn to the stunning views of Gilbertson Pond, Trinity Lakes, and the mountains beyond. "I do love playing this course."

Joel nodded. "Is it true that the course doesn't favor either left or right-handed players?"

Wayne chuckled. "My golf rival in high school was left-handed, and I watched him gain an advantage on many of the courses we played. When we designed the upgraded course, I made sure the right-handed players like myself weren't disadvantaged."

"That's a cool story," Joel said. "My golfing mates back home will like hearing it."

"Do you play much golf?" Wayne asked.

He nodded. "I play many sports. Rowing was my main sport in high school."

"Hannah told me about the rowing connection in England. It's a small world."

"Yes, it is." Joel leaned back in his chair. So far so good.

"Dad, I have a question for you?"

"Sure, sweetheart, what is it?

"I'm looking for information to explain why our lakefront land is zoned as a floodplain."

Wayne's face paled, his eyes widening a fraction before recovering his composure. "I can't remember all the details. I'll ask Sally, my personal assistant, to look through the files on Monday morning."

Hannah's smile brightened. "Thanks, Dad. That would be great."

"No problem. I'll be with Becky on Monday morning. We can talk at lunch before I drive to Spokane to catch the red-eye flight home."

"Lunch will work." She turned to Joel. "Are you planning to stop by for lunch on Monday?"

He shook his head. "I won't have lunch until I'm done with my morning job in town." It was a big job. He'd start early and might need to work through into the afternoon.

Hannah placed her hand over his. "Can you stop by later?"

"Sure." He squeezed her hand, entranced by her sparkling eyes and big smile. Hannah clearly adored her father, and Joel was glad she could spend time with her dad.

Becky returned with drinks and the girls chatted with Wayne. Joel sat back and listened, adding the occasional comment when the girls remembered he existed. Club members stopped by at regular intervals, shaking hands with Wayne, and welcoming him back to his hometown.

Wayne exuded charm and reminded him of Mike. Both Wayne and Mike had that elusive X factor that came from a quiet confidence in their abilities combined with monetary success and accolades in their chosen profession.

Hannah glanced at her phone. "We need to get moving so we have time to shower and change for dinner."

Joel nodded, resisting the temptation to roll his eyes. Yet another change of clothes today. This time he'd iron a collared shirt, and switch to dress shoes.

He wheeled Hannah's golf bag behind him with one hand, held her hand in the other, and walked with her to her SUV.

"I survived meeting your dad." He was grateful their first meeting went well.

"Of course you did. Dad isn't like Mom, and even the long-time club members stopped by to say hello."

"He was Mr. Popularity. I guess you're used to the attention."

She nodded. "Dad's the hometown boy success story, who grew up poor and lived the American dream."

"Does your father have family in town?"

"I don't think so. It won't surprise you to hear that Mom wouldn't let us associate with the people she calls the poor relations."

Wow. "Did you seek out your family? Look them up and try to connect."

Hannah reached her SUV and beeped it open. "With Mom, we choose our battles. Mom insisted we have nothing to do with Dad's relatives."

He shook his head. "I don't understand your family." He couldn't imagine ignoring aunts, uncles, or cousins because of their social status.

"I did warn you that my family is messed up. Mom in particular."

He hoisted Hannah's golf gear into the back of her SUV. "Lucky for you, the state of your family doesn't affect my feelings for you."

Hannah hugged him. "I'm glad to hear this. Mom should be on her best behavior tomorrow."

"I guess that's good news."

"Kind of. She did switch up the schedule with a Mother's Day and birthday brunch instead of the usual dinner. No doubt to stop me and my sisters from spending the day here with Dad."

"She's usually at church on Sunday mornings."

"That's right. She thinks she has one up on Dad. I'm ignoring her little power games."

"I think ignorance regarding anything related to your mother is bliss."

"Which is why Leanna has decided to stay with me instead of Mom."

"Oh boy." There would be drama in her family that he'd try to avoid. He'd seen her father's reaction to her flood zoning question. Wayne knew something, and he looked like he wanted to keep the information buried.

"Grandma will try to manage Mom." She opened the driver's door of her SUV. "Can you be at my place at six?"

"I'll be there." He stole a final kiss. "See you later."

He crossed the parking lot to the far side where he'd left his truck. Hannah drove out of the lot, and he stretched out his arms, releasing tension. He'd thought his family was complicated.

He beeped open his truck and his phone rang. He checked the screen. Mum. Why was she calling? It was already Mother's Day in New Zealand, and they'd planned to chat later this evening.

He answered the call. "Hey Mum, Happy Mother's Day. What's up?"

"I'm at the hospital."

His heart constricted, and he leaned back against his truck. "Are you okay? What happened?"

"It's my knee. We were hiking up Rangitoto and I fell on uneven ground."

"On a path?" If she'd fallen down a ravine …

"Yeah, it was a stupid stumble because I was distracted. We decided to go on a family hike for Mother's Day."

"That's a nice way to spend Mother's Day." Hiking anywhere in New Zealand was amazing, and Rangitoto wasn't an easy hike.

"A great idea in theory, but Bella didn't want to go. She complained the whole time and argued with Mike."

He opened his truck door. The steep mountain climb would have given Bella another reason to whine. "I'm guessing the fighting is what distracted you."

"I don't know what to do with Bella."

"I thought you'd said she'd settled down."

"She was behaving herself until we flew to Auckland. I think she's angry with her father."

Joel swallowed his words. It was futile to mention Bella had a point. Mike was rarely home, and his choices made it clear that his work was more important than his children.

"Joel, are you still there?"

"Sorry, Mum. I'll pray for your knee to heal."

"I need knee replacement surgery ASAP. I'm flying home with Bella and Jack tonight and hoping to book an appointment with my doctor in Sydney on Monday."

"A good idea." It sounded like Mum couldn't delay the surgery.

"Is there any chance you could come home to Australia and help me out? My knee will take time to heal."

He pushed out a long breath and a load of frustration. "I have commitments here. I'm busy with work, then I have vacation time organized for summer camp, then travel plans with the guys."

"Which guys?"

"My mates from the Bible college. We're doing a road trip during their summer break." He couldn't wait to hit the highway and explore the northern states in this beautiful country during the warmer weather.

"But I need you …"

"Actually, I think it's your husband who you need. Why can't Mike work remotely from Australia and assist you?" The million-dollar question his mother wouldn't want to answer.

"It's complicated, Joel. You know that, right? I can pay your airfares and expenses and reimburse your lost income. If I can book in for surgery ASAP, you'd be back in the States in time for summer camp and your road trip."

"Mum, this is a crazy idea. You could hire someone, or a few people, to help you out. My boss needs me at work, and we have customers on a wait list." His boss was happy with the new guy, but there was too much work for one person.

"Sorry, Joel, I have to go. The doctor is here. I'll call you later."

"Take care of yourself, okay. I'll be praying." He ended the call and ran his fingers through his hair. Mum knew which levers to pull to make him feel guilty.

Mike needed to step up and be a father to Bella and Jack. Was it reasonable for Mum to expect Joel to drop everything to help when Mike had the finances and the capacity to fill the void and parent his children?

Joel slid into the driver's seat in his truck. Time away from Australia had given him some unexpected clarity on his mother and her unreasonable requests.

Maybe he should follow Hannah's lead and stand firm on this issue. He wasn't helping Mum by rescuing her from problems that weren't his responsibility to fix.

———

Hannah opened her front door and embraced Leanna in a warm hug. "It's so good to see you."

Leanna stepped back, her suitcase beside her on the porch. "Thanks for letting me stay with no notice."

"I always have room for you. The spare bedroom downstairs is all yours." Dan, on multiple occasions, had snuck into town and stayed with her and Becky without Mom knowing. Grandma couldn't keep a secret of course, and they'd lined up visits for Grandma to see Dan just before he left town.

Hannah settled Leanna in the guest room and padded barefoot into the kitchen. She and Becky had showered and changed, ready for dinner at the country club.

"Ooh la la Hannah! Joel is going to love your dress," Becky said.

She turned in a circle, the blue filmy fabric swirling around her legs. "I'm glad you talked me into buying it."

"It suits you." Becky filled the electric kettle. "Do we have time for tea?"

"We do, because Joel got caught up with something and won't arrive until after six. Dinner is at seven."

"Where are your heels? Which ones are you wearing?"

"My wedge heels, so I won't break my neck."

Becky snickered. "Good plan. The parking lot has too many heel-killing potholes."

"Complain to Dad. It's probably due for resurfacing."

"I might do that. You know, despite how much golf frustrates me, I did make progress with selling Dad on my business plan."

"See." Hannah pulled out a chair at the table. "I told you golf was the secret sauce."

"What matters is Monday morning and showing him why my business is a good investment." Becky removed the lid from the teapot. "Which tea is currently Leanna's favorite?"

"Green tea and jasmine. I'm glad Joel's first meeting with Dad was good."

Becky added loose leaf tea and poured hot water into the pot. "Dad likes him, which doesn't surprise me. We all love Joel."

"Except for Mom." Tomorrow, Joel would be within her mother's orbit of negativity and disparaging remarks.

"Forget about Mom. She's only happy if she has something— or many things—to complain about."

Leanna breezed into the kitchen, wearing a fitted black dress that highlighted her athletic physique. "I want to divorce Mom."

"Don't we all," Becky said.

"Seriously. I can't deal with her neurotic and controlling behavior."

Hannah crossed her legs, adjusting the long skirt over her knees. "She thinks you're having wild and unsupervised parties with teens who don't wear enough clothes."

"Oh, please, that only happened once. It was my friend's birthday, and she invited friends, who invited people who crashed our pool party."

Hannah frowned. "Can you blame Mom for being concerned?"

"I'd already locked up the house. We weren't drinking or doing anything you two wouldn't do. The gate-crashers were out of control, the nosy neighbors called the cops, and Dan got an earful of complaints from everyone."

"Poor Dan." Becky placed three cups next to the teapot. "He kept those details to himself."

"He understood, thankfully. The nosy neighbors are always home and checking up on us, which is kind of working in my favor."

"There had to be a silver lining somewhere." Becky poured tea into the cups.

Leanna dropped into a chair opposite Hannah. "The thing is, my friends are nerdy and desperate for good grades. Dan's house is quiet, even when he's home, and it's where we escape the dorm to study and exercise in the pool and play tennis. And cook ourselves proper meals in his amazing kitchen."

"His kitchen is cool." Hannah had kitchen envy, and she'd thought about remodeling her own kitchen.

"Anyway, Mom is being overly dramatic, and I told her I'd had enough. I'm flying back tomorrow night in time for my classes on Monday afternoon."

"A good idea." Becky brought their cups to the table and claimed a seat.

Hannah patted Leanna's hand. "Becky and I can try and smooth things over with Mom."

Leanna cracked a small smile. "I appreciate you both. I'm glad Dad is less complicated than Mom."

"Actually, I'm not so sure about that." Hannah lifted her teacup, inhaling the relaxing scent.

Becky whipped her head around, staring wide eyed at Hannah. "Am I hearing you right? Are you secretly having issues with Dad?"

Hannah let out a frustrated sigh. "I don't know what to think." She filled her sisters in on Tabby's questions and the information from Robert.

Leanna's face fell, as if she had the weight of the world on her lean shoulders. "You can't possibly think Dad might have done something dodgy. There must be another reason."

Becky carried the pot of tea to the table and topped up her cup. "I can believe Dad would do something that gave him an advantage."

"No Becky. You're way off base," Hannah said.

"Am I? I saw Dad's ruthless side when he cut off my trust fund."

"To be fair ..." Leanna paused, teacup in mid-air. "You did quit college and refuse to compromise or look at alternative courses."

Becky stared into her teacup, as if it held the answers to her problems. "I'm just saying business is a cutthroat world that rewards ruthless behavior. There may be a noble reason to explain why Dad made a gray-area decision that's legal but might be considered unfair or unethical."

Hannah shook her head. "I'm with Leanna. I can't believe you're saying this about Dad."

Becky crossed her arms over her torso, her mouth set in a determined line. "Remember what Mom said, years ago. She claimed Dad had done bad stuff."

"But Mom never gave us details. She never produced any evidence to prove anything." Hannah was convinced the "bad stuff" didn't exist. Mom had been bluffing, trying to turn them against Dad.

"And it's not because Dan didn't try to work out what really happened," Leanna said. "When push came to shove, Mom shut up."

Hannah sipped her tea. "I'm giving Dad the benefit of the doubt. I'll see what he says on Monday."

Dad had appeared confident that he could locate the files containing the information she'd requested. She prayed there was a simple explanation that would allow Tabby's family to make the most of their lakefront land.

CHAPTER TEN

The next morning, Hannah held Joel's hand and drew comfort from his presence as they followed her sisters up the front steps at her mother's house. The family home, where Hannah had grown up, was set back from the road, and spread over an acre of spacious grounds. Grandma had her own wing, the size of a large studio apartment, on the lower level at the back. She had fantastic views of Trinity Lakes and the mountains. Visitor parking spaces were plentiful on the long circular drive.

Joel squeezed her hand. "We can do this."

"I'm praying we'll survive." Mom had decided brunch wasn't good enough for her birthday party and Mother's Day celebrations. She'd hired a catering firm to set up a marquee on the lawn next to her prized rose garden and serve high tea.

Grandma greeted them at the front door and lapped up all their loving and genuine happy Grandmother day gifts and good wishes. "If only Dan was here, I'd have all my grandchildren together."

"How is Mom today?" Hannah asked.

"She's in a good mood, and she's happy the weather is sunny."

Hannah let out the breath she wasn't aware she was holding. Tension and stress were her constant companion now Dad and Leanna were in town. Thank goodness for the blessing of fine weather.

"Your mother asked me to direct our guests to walk around the back to the rose garden."

Becky nodded. "Is there anything we can do to help?"

"No, my dear." Grandma's content smile made up for all the angst. "Flatter your mother with birthday greetings and gifts, and pray she can behave herself for the next two hours."

Leanna sighed. "I'll hide in the rose garden and count down the minutes until I can leave. Did you know she forbade me from requesting a glass of her expensive French champagne?"

Hannah's brows shot up. "Mom's serving alcohol. Really?"

"Apparently that's how one serves A Proper English High Tea," Grandma said in her best Lady of the Manor voice.

"But Mom doesn't drink alcohol." Hannah had endured frequent annoying lectures about the perils of alcohol during her teen years.

"At three hundred dollars a bottle, it's unlikely anyone will be served enough champagne to become drunk at this early hour." A hint of mischief in Grandma's smile gave the game away. "Susannah may not drink alcohol in front of her children. What she does behind closed doors …"

"Wow." Hannah shook her head.

Becky rolled her eyes. "Why doesn't this surprise me?"

Mom's hypocrisy was reaching new heights, after preaching abstinence at all costs for years. Instead of going to church, Mom would be sipping champagne with her posh church lady friends. Lovely.

Joel turned to face her, his hand on her cheek. "You sure you're okay?"

She nodded. "I try to forget Mom is a hypocrite. Do as I say, not as I do."

"Expensive champagne is not my jam," he said. "We can decline the bubbly and make the most of the high tea. The food is usually good."

She tipped her head to the side. "You know about high tea."

He grinned. "Cucumber sandwiches and English scones with jam and cream. Plus mini desserts and hot tea. A smorgasbord of food in small quantities."

"Okay, I'm sold, and I'll stay by your side."

"An excellent plan."

They followed Becky and Leanna along the path around the side of the house. An enormous back deck opened out onto a green lawn which sloped down into the garden. A large white marquee was set up on a flat area of lawn next to the colorful flowers in the rose garden.

"Please tell me Gracie doesn't do all the gardening herself."

Hannah chuckled. "The gardener's here at least once a week."

"I'm relieved to hear that."

She pointed to a garden bed of tulips and irises nearing the end of their season. "Grandma and Mom fuss over the flower beds and the rose garden. The gardener takes care of the lawn and does most of the planting and work in the veggie and herb gardens. I think Grandma still insists on pruning the fruit trees."

"It's a big job, looking after a property this size."

"It's too big for Mom and Grandma, but Mom won't consider downsizing." The status from living in one of the premier homes at the top of the hill was important to her mother.

He looked around. "The views are stunning, and the gardens are beautiful."

"True. My quarter-acre plot is big enough for me. I remember this house being built when I was a child. Dad redeveloped the country club estate, and that's when this housing estate was built."

"I'm assuming the hill used to be farmland?"

She nodded. "The original entry to the golf course was along a lane by the river that no longer exists. The old road wasn't far from the bridge where we had lunch after kayaking the rivers."

"Interesting. Your father would've needed a lot of money to invest in building the country club and new golf course."

"It was expensive but ultimately profitable. He invested his earnings and sponsorship money from the tour and built his dream."

Taking into account all the time and money Dad had invested in Trinity Lakes, it was interesting he'd hardly spent any time here over the last decade. Divorcing Mom had soured his pleasure in visiting his hometown.

"Your father has great weather today for the golf tournament."

"I'm glad." Dad was sponsoring a golf tournament for special needs athletes this morning. The event had attracted players from all over Washington, and nearby states. A section of the golf course by the river was visible in the distance. She wished she was there instead of being stuck at Mom's party.

They crossed the lawn and joined a line to enter the marquee.

Hannah stood in line, her hand tucked within Joel's firm grasp. She greeted many of the fifty invited guests, introducing them to Joel while they waited.

This was a small gathering by her mother's standards. A gift table was set up near Mom's table at the front. Mom had informed her, via a curt message, that Mom would be sitting with Grandma and two of their friends.

Hannah and Joel reached the front of the line, and Mom gave them a big smile. Her brief hugs and air kisses kept up the happy family appearance.

Mom opened the gift box from Hannah, plucking out a gift card from Hannah's favorite store. "Thank you. I'll enjoy browsing the shelves to find new books."

"I can give you some recommendations," Hannah said.

"Yes, please. I've almost finished reading my ninth regency romance from Carolyn Miller."

Hannah nodded. "I knew you'd love her books."

"The beautiful stories, and the house parties on the country estates, inspired me to create an English garden party theme."

Hannah chuckled. "Shall I call you Lady Gilbertson?" She could play along with the public charade of goodwill for their audience.

"No, my dear. I think I'm more suited to being a duchess."

"As you wish." If Mom had been born in England, she'd have set her sights on marrying a wealthy duke.

Joel cleared his throat. "Your gardens are lovely, and perfect for high tea."

"Thank you. My roses are doing well this year."

Hannah wound up their conversation and moved forward with Joel to view the seating plan. Allocated seating was mandatory at Mom's events. They were banished to Mom's equivalent of the servant quarters, a table for four with Becky and Leanna on the far side of the marquee. A blessing, rather than a punishment, if Mom was in one of her moods.

Joel whispered in her ear. "Everything seems to be going well."

"Yes." Too well for her liking. When Mom was being charming and sweet, it was inevitable that something would happen to break the illusion of the perfect and harmonious family. Hannah prayed she was wrong.

———

JOEL SIPPED French Earl Grey tea from a delicate floral teacup. Hannah and her sisters were chatting away, their voices soft to prevent guests at nearby tables from eavesdropping.

He enjoyed a small triangle sandwich with smoked salmon and cream cheese. Mum would love this party. Classical music played in the background, and a single short-stemmed apricot rose in a skinny crystal vase on their table added to the lingering rose scent from the fragrant garden.

He'd snapped a few photos on his phone of the three-tiered centerpiece plates loaded with sweet and savory treats, and photos of Hannah with her sisters. Hannah had insisted they add a couple of selfies to their growing Joel-and-Hannah photo collection.

The music faded, and Susannah addressed her guests from the front of the gathering. He clapped at the appropriate times and joined in the singing of the traditional happy birthday song.

Gracie and a few ladies he recognized from his occasional visits to Sunday morning church services gave short speeches and compliments to Susannah.

Becky had been chosen to speak on behalf of her siblings. Hannah hadn't said anything, but he could tell she was upset by the blatant snub. Leanna, on the other hand, would struggle to hold a civil conversation with Susannah.

In true middle child style, Becky was conciliatory, witty, and entertaining in her remarks.

The formalities ended, and Joel turned to Hannah. "That wasn't so bad."

Hannah's lower lip trembled, and he wished he could smooth away the creases between her brows. Her eyes were glassy, and she rapidly blinked away the tears building in her eyes. "I'm sorry, Joel."

"You have no reason to apologize."

"My mother ... she's always included me and Leanna in any speeches."

He suppressed the anger that matched the fire in Leanna's low volume conversation with Becky. The sisters weren't born yesterday, and they understood Susannah's coded message. "Hannah, this isn't your fault. It's your mother's choice, and her baggage."

Hannah held his gaze. "Thanks for being here."

"I wouldn't want to be anywhere else." The subtle pressure exerted by Susannah had backfired, and his relationship with Hannah was growing stronger every day.

The sisters had cleaned up the food, only crumbs remaining on their floral-patterned tea plates.

Leanna topped up her teacup from a matching floral teapot. "When I finish my tea, we can hide in the rose garden."

Becky snickered. "The garden isn't that big, and everyone will be mingling there."

"I can still try," Leanna said. "I told Mom I'd make a scene if she cornered me."

"No." Hannah's wide eyes revealed her dismay. "This is Mom's day. Please don't provoke her."

"She publicly snubbed us by only letting Becky talk." Leanna folded her arms over her torso. "I've run out of patience."

"Leanna, let it go," Becky said. "It's not worth it."

Leanna finished her tea and stood. "If you all insist I have to keep my mouth shut, then I need to take a walk."

Joel stood and cupped Hannah's elbow as they followed the group into the rose garden. He loosened the tie he'd worn over his button-up white shirt. The party would be winding up soon, and he could remove the tie that choked his neck.

Hannah linked her fingers through his and leaned into his side. "I'm relieved the party has gone better than expected."

"I'm glad you're happy." He missed the simplicity of his family. If someone had a problem, they hashed it out with the people involved and worked out a compromise. Susannah's mind games were childish and annoying.

Hannah paused and leaned toward a vibrant yellow rose. "This smells divine, but I drank too much tea. I need to duck inside and use the restroom."

"I can walk with you."

"No, please enjoy the rose garden. I'll be back soon."

He nodded, let go of her hand, and watched her stride toward the house. The skirt of her long floral dress floated around her legs in the light breeze.

A delicate cough distracted him from his vision of his beautiful Hannah. He turned around and stared into Susannah's icy pale blue eyes.

"Happy birthday." He said the first and only thing that came to mind.

"Yes." Susannah kept her wide smile in place, but her quiet tone had a hard edge that mirrored her eyes. "My birthday will be happy when you break up with Hannah and go back to Australia."

Her low blow was like a sharp punch to his solar plexus. He schooled his features into a neutral expression and stared her down. He'd never liked bullies, and he'd keep his emotions in check.

"Mrs. Gilbertson, I'm sorry you've chosen this hill to die on. Your happiness is your problem."

Her face flamed red, and she stood taller, hands on hips. "How dare you defy me. Please leave. Now."

"How dare you try to bully me. I know your type, and you don't scare me."

Susannah stamped her foot. "Leave now, or I'll make a scene."

"No you won't." He held back a laugh, attempting to hide his amusement at her toddler tantrum. "People are watching, and you care too much about what other people think."

"Hannah is making a big mistake." Her voice lifted, her anger and agitation resonating in every word. "I'll never accept you as part of my family."

"That's your loss." He spun on his heel and power walked toward the house. He was done with her immature games and phony behavior. At least he knew where he stood with Susannah.

"Joel!" Becky caught up to him. "Where are you going?"

"To find Hannah. I've been ordered off the property."

Becky muttered a few choice words under her breath. "She told you to break up with Hannah, didn't she?"

He nodded. "It wasn't unexpected to hear your mother spell out her birthday wish."

"Oh Joel, please don't give up on Hannah. Don't let my mother win."

Becky's words highlighted the stupidity of the situation. Hannah couldn't win. Her mother had played her hand, and was forcing Hannah to make a painful choice. Joel prayed for wisdom, and prayed for a solution that wouldn't break Hannah's beautiful heart.

———

ON MONDAY MORNING, Hannah was swamped with a long to-do list at the rowing club. Taking a whole weekend off was a luxury, and the administrative backlog took time to clear.

Being busy, with her mind occupied, was a blessing after the fiasco of Mom's party yesterday morning. Hannah resented Mom's interference in her life. It wasn't fair. Why couldn't Mom be happy for her?

Hannah leaned back in her desk chair, rubbing her fingers over her aching forehead and temples. She'd take another painkiller at lunch, once she had some food in her stomach. Not that she had much of an appetite today.

Yesterday afternoon had been an improvement on the

morning. Hannah had stood with Joel, applauding the special needs golfers as they received their medals. Her father had conducted the low-key and informal ceremony in the outdoor restaurant seating area at the country club.

The aroma of beef patties cooking on the grill had wafted in the air. A production line of volunteers had manned the tables where the athletes and supporters collected their lunch.

Hannah let out a frustrated breath. If only she'd been at the country club yesterday morning, helping Dad on the golf course as an official, instead of attending her mother's decadent high tea. When Joel had caught up with her at the house and repeated Mom's outrageous demands, Hannah had used every ounce of self-control to leave the party without losing it and confronting Mom.

She'd let her tears flow when Joel had dropped her home after Mom's party. They'd both gone home to change into golf attire for their round with Dad in the afternoon. At least the golf had gone well. Dad was his usual, easygoing self, who'd made Joel feel welcome.

Yesterday's beautiful weather had disappeared. It was humid this morning, and dark clouds had formed over the mountains. Sometimes the early summer storms stayed in the mountains and moved away to the east. She'd check the weather forecast during lunch and, if necessary, cancel their afternoon bookings.

Hannah had prioritized time this morning to do an online search of the town records. Her father had been mayor when the zoning change had taken place. Hopefully he would solve the mystery at lunch, and provide the information Tabby's family would need if they intended to review the current zoning of their lakefront land.

Hannah finished her tepid coffee. She'd only stopped for a few minutes earlier to chat with Grandma, who was thankfully unaware of Mom's conversation with Joel. Grandma had been excited because she'd visited with a friend who served

Australian Afternoon Tea. She'd liked the flavor and had ordered it online. Grandma looked forward to sharing an afternoon pot of tea with Joel. If only tea was Hannah's biggest concern.

Her phone beeped. Becky had packed up early and was bringing leftover pies and pastries to the rowing club for lunch. Her morning with Dad had gone well, and Dad had helped Becky behind the counter by serving customers. Hannah needed to hear that good news. It served as a reminder that Dad was still in her corner.

She checked the time on her phone. Tabby started work in an hour. Hannah prayed she'd have answers and some good news from Dad to share with Tabby.

Hannah left her office and headed to the kitchen. She collected plates, napkins, and ketchup from the cupboards. Earlier she'd moved a table to the undercover veranda and changed into her kayaking gear.

Joel should be finished at his tiling job in town. He'd ordered a burger for lunch from the Bellbird, and said he'd kayak with Hannah after lunch if the weather stayed fine.

Hannah couldn't blame him for declining her lunch invitation and wanting a break from her family. Joel hadn't said much, but she could tell Mom's behavior had hurt him. His own mother in Australia had knee surgery scheduled for later this week. She could understand why Joel was preoccupied and concerned about his family, especially his sister.

Becky and Dad arrived, and they helped her set up lunch on the veranda. Hannah chose an Aussie beef pie and added ketchup on top.

Becky smiled. "This is nice, the three of us having lunch."

"Yes." Dad poured iced tea into a glass. "The weather isn't looking good though."

The rain clouds had rolled in overhead, releasing the occasional light sprinkle of rain.

"I'm hoping the storm stays in the mountains." If the storm shifted their way, Hannah would need to move equipment into the shed, and cancel the afternoon bookings.

"I closed early, just in case." Becky selected a mini quiche. "I've been caught out before with a fast-moving storm front, and it's not fun."

Hannah finished her pie and switched her attention to Dad. "What's the deal with the land zoning?"

"It's complicated." He took another bite from his pie, taking his sweet time to answer. "When I was mayor, there was a developer who wanted to buy all the lakefront land."

"Really?" Becky paused, her quiche mid-air. "I don't remember hearing about this."

Dad placed his pie on his plate. "It was kept quiet. No one in Trinity Lakes wanted a massive lakefront hotel and resort complex. The developer wanted to move the lakefront road and circle it behind the campground to allow space for a mall."

"Wow." Hannah looked at the pristine lake and surrounding parkland. "A development of that size would have destroyed Trinity Lakes."

Dad nodded. "They also proposed a large housing estate development on this side of town to accommodate the influx of workers."

"I can understand why people were against the development. But why was the zoning changed to a floodplain?" Hannah asked.

Dad finished his pie before answering. "Hannah, I know you like to believe the best in people. This developer was successful in other parts of the Northwest precisely because they didn't care about what the townsfolk thought or wanted."

Becky wrinkled her nose. "But to do any development, they had to convince someone to sell them the land."

"And that was the problem we faced," Dad said. "Circumstances meant the previous owner of this land needed to sell quickly. They couldn't afford to turn down any offers."

"But you haven't answered my question." The history lesson was interesting, but not necessarily relevant. "Why the zoning change?"

Dad sighed. "It was the only way. We had to do something."

Becky narrowed her eyes. "What do you mean by we? Who else was involved?"

"It doesn't matter," he said. "I could afford to buy the undeveloped land, but I couldn't match the price offered by the developer."

Hannah sat taller, straightening her spine, her mind swirling and drawing unwanted conclusions. Who else was involved in this shady deal? "What exactly are you saying, Dad?"

"The developer withdrew their offer to purchase the land when the zoning amendment came into effect."

Hannah gasped. "Is this land a floodplain, or not? Yes or no."

Her father shrugged. "That question isn't important."

"How can you say that?" Hannah shook her head, perplexed by her father's evasive answers. "What's the truth?"

"Hannah, what's important is that the development was stopped. That's what mattered."

Her pounding headache escalated into migraine territory. "Dad, why can't you give me a straight answer?"

"It was a complex and difficult situation because the negative consequences from their development plans were massive. The rowing and sailing clubs would be gone. The kids in town would have lost access to the best section of the lake for rowing training. Remember Richie, Dan's friend? His parents couldn't afford his college tuition without a sports scholarship, so he needed to row. You would never have been able to even start rowing if we'd let the development go forward."

No. She must be hearing Dad wrong. This couldn't be true.

"Where's the paperwork and the environmental studies to confirm the land is a floodplain?"

He shrugged. "I've no clue. What I do know is when the zoning change was proposed, none of the impacted landowners lodged a formal objection."

"Not even the original owner of this land?" Becky asked. "They must have lost a chunk of money by selling to you instead of the developer."

Dad crossed his arms over his chest, his gaze defiant. "They didn't need or want billions. My offer more than covered what they needed. And no one wanted to see the town and surrounding environment ruined."

"Let me get this straight." Hannah held Dad's unwavering gaze, seeking answers he didn't appear to want to give. "Is this land really a floodplain?"

"All land has the potential to flood. Especially waterfront land." He raised his hands in the air. "Honestly, Hannah, I don't know why you're making this into a big deal."

What? How could Dad be cavalier and dismissive of this important issue? "It's a big deal for Tabby's family. What if they want to develop the old boat shed site?"

"Good for them." Dad kept his smile intact, his tone softer and conciliatory. "A town zoning decision can be reversed if the right evidence is provided."

The right evidence. Like the so-called evidence from twenty years ago that couldn't be found. If it ever existed?

Her mind raced in circles, like a spinning top that wouldn't stop turning. Would Dad give her a straight answer? "Do we legitimately own this land?"

"Of course we do. Sweetheart, don't worry about what happened twenty years ago. It doesn't matter."

It mattered to her. She braced her hands on the table, his words feeling like a dagger shoved deep into her stomach. He'd withheld important information regarding assets in her trust fund. Her pulse kicked up another notch, the pounding in her head a persistent drumbeat that wouldn't stop.

Dad had dodged her questions. Robert's words from their phone call swirled in her mind. Dad hadn't reassured her that the zoning change and his subsequent purchase of the land was a hundred percent legitimate. Dad had broken her trust and behaved like Mom. It was too much.

She pushed back her chair. "I need space."

"Hannah. Where are you going?" Becky asked.

Hannah ignored her sister and collected her pink vest from the hook behind her office door. She grabbed the keys from her desk drawer and jogged to the side entrance, racing around to the shed and the roller door where she stored her kayak. Big rain drops cooled the aggravation heating her face.

Becky huffed and puffed and followed her into the boat shed. "What are you doing? You can't go kayaking by yourself in this weather."

She tossed the keys to Becky. "Tabby will arrive soon. I'm clocking off."

"Hannah, no. Please talk to me."

"Later." She clicked her vest into place, picked up her kayak, and ran to the water's edge. She shoved the kayak into the gray water, then hopped inside in one fluid motion before Becky even reached the shoreline.

"Hannah. Please. Don't do this!" Becky stood at the water's edge, yelling and begging her to return to shore.

She ignored Becky and stroked through the water, the rain pitter-pattering on her pink kayak. Old habits led her to follow a training route toward the bridge.

Hot tears joined the cool raindrops streaking her cheeks. First Mom and now Dad had lied to her and broken their promises. Mom had promised she'd be nice to Joel at her party. Dad had assured her he'd always be honest and tell her the truth.

Had Dad cheated the owner by offering a lower price after the flood zoning took effect? Was her trust fund, and her life's work, built on a lie?

Hannah stroked harder and faster, not caring which direction she took. How could Dad do this to her? Could her trust fund be in legal hot water due to her father's actions?

She pushed the paddle harder, the rain pounding her body. Trinity Lakes was her home, the one place in the world where she belonged. Dad had lied to her by omission, refusing to reveal the whole truth. She wanted to escape and pretend the last few days were a bad dream rather than a living nightmare.

CHAPTER ELEVEN

At lunchtime on Monday, Joel sat by himself on a park bench in the Village Green on Main Street. He swallowed the last delicious bite of his Aussie-style burger. The Bellbird had made his beef burger to order, and included cheddar cheese, crispy bacon, a fried egg, and slices of pineapple and beetroot. A taste of home on a day when he was feeling homesick for his family.

The weather matched his mood. Gray clouds were becoming denser and blocking the sun. The birds overhead in the trees were squawking and carrying on, a sure sign the weather was shifting.

Chatter in the café had focused on the storm and heavy rainfall expected to hit Trinity Lakes within the next few hours. He'd changed into kayaking gear before lunch, figuring waterproof clothing would be helpful in the rain even if kayaking with Hannah was canceled.

He checked his phone messages. Mum again. Mike wouldn't fly back to Australia to help Mum on Friday when her knee surgery was scheduled. Not even to look after Bella and Jack.

Joel replied to Mum with consoling words that differed to

his thoughts. How could Mike's work be more important? At least Bella had calmed down now she was back home in Sydney. Who knew how long her good behavior would last?

His phone rang. Becky. Why would she be calling?

He answered the call. "Hey, Becky."

"Joel, where are you?" Becky's panicked tone snagged his attention.

"The Village Green. Why?"

"Please hurry to the rowing club. Hannah needs you."

"Okay." He collected his belongings and started walking to his truck parked on Main Street near the Bellbird. "What happened?"

"She's upset and she took off. Kayaking."

His pulse rate leaped higher, and he picked up his pace, worried about Hannah. The temperature had dropped, and a misty rain shower had everyone on Main Street scurrying indoors or into their vehicles. "I'm near my truck. Hang on, and I'll put you through the speakers."

He climbed into his truck and started the engine. Of course, Main Street was now full of vehicles on the move.

"Joel, are you there?"

"Yeah, there's a traffic jam on Main Street. I'll be there soon. Why's Hannah upset?"

Becky filled him in on her lunch conversation with Hannah and Dad.

"So your father lied to Hannah."

"To be fair, he had good reasons. Dad made sure a developer couldn't buy the land and ruin Trinity Lakes. It's not like he was motivated by greed."

"But Hannah isn't seeing it his way." Oh boy, this wasn't going to end well. Hannah adored her father, and he'd toppled off his pedestal in front of her eyes.

"Dad loves this town, Joel."

"That's not the issue."

"Dad could have invested in a different project and made a lot more money. And whoever owned the land would have made a lot more money if they'd sold to the developer."

"Maybe." He reversed his truck into a gap in the traffic and crawled along Main Street. "I'm guessing Hannah's feeling betrayed by your dad. He's broken her trust by withholding information."

"I can't deny that's true."

"Then you can understand why Hannah's upset."

"Yes, of course I can. But, according to Dad, the town Hannah loves wouldn't exist if the developers had bought the land. I can see the logic behind Dad's decision, even if I hate how he handled it."

Hannah had more at stake than Becky. It wasn't Becky's trust fund and career that was caught up in events from twenty-something years ago.

"I'm minutes away," he said. "Can you see Hannah on the lake?"

"Give me a minute. Dad's on the dock with Grandma's bird-watching binoculars tracking her route. I'm getting your kayak and gear ready."

"Thanks." The windscreen wipers flipped forward and back, the rain becoming heavier as he drove closer to the rowing club.

"She's still in sight. Are you wearing kayaking gear?"

"Thankfully, yes."

"Good. I have everything you'll need on the veranda."

"Okay, I'll be there in a few minutes." He disconnected the call, glad his phone was charged. He prayed he'd catch up with Hannah on the lake so he could convince her to talk with him somewhere dry and out of the rain.

He pulled into a parking spot and jogged to the rowing club veranda. Hannah was in her pink kayak on the far side of the lake, thrashing her paddle through the water. There was palpable anger in every fierce stroke.

The outer layer of his rain jacket was wet from the solid downpour. He climbed the veranda steps, water dripping off his jacket as he greeted Becky.

"I'm glad you're here." Relief flooded Becky's face. "If I was better at kayaking, I'd try to chase her down myself."

"Is Tabby here?"

Becky shook her head. "She will be soon."

Hannah must be distraught to abandon the rowing club and leave Becky in charge.

"I can get you a dry jacket," Becky said.

"I'm good." He picked up the waterproof bags Becky had packed. "Let's do this."

Wayne met him at the boat shed. "Please tell Hannah I love her and I'm sorry. We did what had to be done to save the town."

Joel nodded. "Is there anything else I need to know?"

"She's not answering her phone." Wayne wiped rainwater off his face. "She may be ignoring me, or she may have forgotten her phone."

"Okay. I've got my phone. I'll be in touch."

Wayne nodded. "Thank you."

"I'll be praying," Becky said.

"Thanks." He launched his kayak into the choppy water and paddled toward the middle of the lake. Visibility was sketchy and he was glad Hannah wore bright pink.

Hannah was paddling fast, in the direction of the mountains. Surely she wasn't going to kayak into the river? The swollen river, combined with the stormwater, was a disaster waiting to happen.

Joel swung around, kayaking along the southern shore toward the river. Hannah was ahead, too far ahead to hear him call out. Had she seen him following her?

He powered on, grateful he knew the flow of the lake currents and the fastest way to try and catch her. She was on a mission, head down, arms whipping up foamy water as she gained speed, the lake current pulling her toward the river.

Lightning lit up the sky and thunder cracked through the air. This storm was a doozy, and it wasn't safe on the water.

Joel's heart rate accelerated, his arm muscles burning. Fear and despair tore him apart. She was committed to kayaking the river. The rapids would be dangerous, a death trap for even an experienced kayaker. He prayed Hannah would change course before it was too late.

HANNAH SHIVERED. The cool rainwater felt like a shower of grenades pounding her head. Her arm muscles ached, and she lifted her head. Where was she on the lake?

She glanced around and gulped. The swollen river dragged her forward, pushing her kayak toward the rapids. Tree branches and other debris floated in the muddy water. How far along the river had she traveled?

She stared at the water ahead, desperate to calm her mind. Think. Pray. Don't give in to the panic. There must be a way to get up on the riverbank before she reached the rapids.

The current pulled her around a bend. Ahead was a section of cleared land on the riverbank. She prayed for a burst of energy and the physical strength to paddle diagonally across the current to the shore.

Hannah gritted her teeth and dug in deep. Her life was on the line if she couldn't make it to shore. She darted around a log, avoiding a collision by only a few feet. Pain shot through her body, and she braced for a rough landing on the riverbank.

Her kayak scraped over the muddy bank, sliding to a halt beside a tree. She sucked in deep breaths and whispered a prayer of thanks. She was safe.

Hannah stepped out of the kayak, her legs unsteady on the

muddy ground. She dropped to her knees and pulled her kayak higher up on the riverbank. Somehow it had escaped being damaged during her harrowing ride along the river.

The river currents rushed by, and the rain eased. The rain stopped, and she looked around, desperate to see a familiar landmark.

Her hopes faded. She was lost. Her phone was in her office drawer. She didn't have her dry pack with her, or any way to communicate with the outside world.

A kayaker wearing yellow came into view. Joel? Yes, Joel. Thank goodness. She screamed and yelled and waved her arms in the air, praying he'd make a smooth landing on shore.

Her heart leapt into her throat and threatened to explode, as if a spray of bullets had penetrated its core. Fear choked her neck, circling her like an army marching in toward its target. If Joel died, it would be her fault.

He paddled hard, his strong arms and shoulders directing his kayak to the riverbank. The nose of the kayak lifted in the air and crash landed in the mud.

His kayak slid to a halt in front of hers, only a few feet from the rushing water. He anchored his paddle in the mud and stood.

"Joel!" She ran to him, throwing her arms around his solid body. "You're safe."

"Yeah." His arms held her close. "You scared me."

"Sorry." A fresh wave of tears streaked her face. She helped him out of the kayak, and they pulled it higher on the bank.

He cupped her face, staring into her eyes. "We need to get warm and get help."

"I've got nothing. Not even my phone."

He cracked a smile, muddy rivers of dirt smeared over his cheeks. "Becky packed supplies."

"I love my sister." She opened a bag and pulled out a first aid kit and two thermal blankets. "This will help."

"It will." He tossed her a pink lightweight zip hoodie and a dry pair of thick socks. "Becky is a lifesaver."

"She is." Hannah moved her kayak away from the tree, using it as a seat. She swapped her wet jacket for the hoodie, pulled off her soggy shoes, and attempted to towel her tangled wet hair dry.

She wrapped the thermal blanket around her body and pulled on the thick socks. Warmth spread through her torso and feet, bringing her hope.

Joel followed Hannah's lead, shedding his rain jacket, and wrapping the blanket around his shoulders. He sat beside her on his kayak and held his phone, his gaze focused on the screen.

"Is there a signal?" she asked.

"It's weak, only one bar. I've sent Becky a text with our map coordinates."

She sipped water and nibbled on a protein bar she'd found in the bag. The compass app in his phone had come in handy. "Where exactly are we?"

"Not far from the back road to the highway. A mile north of the rapids."

Only a mile. Thank you, Jesus. If she hadn't looked up and paid attention to her surroundings ...

"Joel, I'm sorry. This is all my fault."

"It's okay." He checked his phone. "ETA is at least an hour, unless the mountain rescue crew can assist."

"That's good news, right?"

He switched off his phone. "We're not safe here."

"What? Why?" Panic choked her throat.

He put his blanket and gear in his kayak. "The water is rising. We have to move to higher ground ASAP."

She stared at the rushing water. "Has the river broken its bank?"

He nodded. "It rained all weekend in the mountains. They said floodwaters are heading our way."

"What about the kayaks?"

"We keep them with us, just in case …"

Could they avoid the rising floodwaters? Hannah silently prayed while she pulled off her dry hoodie and warm socks, tossing them and the blanket back into the dry bag, and into her kayak.

She put on her soggy shoes, globs of mud squishing between her toes. Ew. But gross muddy shoes would provide better grip than bare feet.

The ground ahead was a gentle uphill slope, too slick for walking. She crawled on her knees, pushing her kayak ahead of her. using her knees and the tips of her shoes to grip the sodden ground. It was a slow process.

Joel crawled beside her, pushing his kayak forward up the muddy bank. "You okay?"

"Yeah. This slope is steeper than it looks." Sunshine baked the river mud into her skin. At least the itchy mud would protect her skin from sunburn and bugs.

"It sure is. Not far to go."

"Can we walk when we reach the top?" She didn't want to slip and slide down the bank and into the river.

"I hope so. They said we'll see a picnic area. That's where we shelter until help arrives."

"Sounds good." A light at the end of a long muddy climb. She drew in deep breaths and heaved the kayak forward. Inch by inch, they moved closer to safety.

She pushed her kayak over the crest of the hill and collapsed on her stomach. Fatigue and adrenaline fought for supremacy. Bone weary tired didn't begin to describe her exhaustion, although her headache had eased.

"Hannah, are you all right?"

She turned her head to the side and opened her eyes. Joel kneeled beside her, his eyes full of concern.

"How far to shelter?" she whispered.

"Less than a hundred feet. Rest, and I'll move our gear."

"Okay." Her eyelids were heavy, and the pull of sleep irresistible.

She rolled over, but a rock dug into her side and jolted her awake.

"Hold on," Joel said.

He placed one arm under her back and the other under her knees, lifting her into his muscular arms.

She nestled into his chest, drawing comfort from his nearness. It felt good and right to be held in his arms. The swamp smell lingered, but she didn't care. They were alive and safe, and her stupid, impulsive behavior hadn't injured either of them.

A familiar picnic area appeared. "I know where we are. This was a training stop."

"That's good. Now we wait."

He lowered her to her feet, and she sank onto the bench, her back resting against the edge of the table. "Solid ground is good. I've never seen the river this high here."

He nodded and pulled his phone out of his kayak. "I'll message our updated map coordinates to search and rescue."

His phone pinged. "Have they replied?" she asked.

"We're in the right place, and they asked us to wait for the rescue team."

"Was the storm bad?"

"Yeah, although we've somehow missed the worst of it. There's flash flooding along the rivers and in the low-lying parts of town."

"Oh no, I hope everyone is okay." Spring rains added more water to the rivers, and the lakes could fill to overflowing.

"Me, too. They're busy with callouts in town, mainly from fallen trees."

"But it hasn't been windy," she said.

He nodded. "Becky said high winds were a problem on the

other side of town. A fast-moving storm cell from the north joined the mountain storm and wreaked havoc."

"That's terrible news." The farms and ranches out of town needed rain, but they could do without the storms.

"That's why mountain rescue will be helping us." He placed their gear on the table.

She pulled off her shoes and found a small dry towel in the bag, along with a spare pair of sneakers. Her hoodie and socks kept her warm, and she stretched out her legs along the length of the bench seat.

Joel sat on the other side of the table, looking weary.

She tossed him a container of bear spray. "Just in case."

"Really? You think there's bears out and about."

"We can't be too careful." The thought of bears distracted her from the real reason why they were stuck in the wilderness.

He drank from his water bottle. "I'm glad I had a big lunch."

"You're not hungry?"

He shook his head, his gaze on his phone screen. "Becky sends her love and wants you to listen to me. And do what I say."

She groaned. "I can hear her lecture in my head."

He paused, his gaze soft. "Do you want to talk about it?"

"Not really." She clenched her hands together, holding back tears. "Did Becky mention what happened at lunch?"

He nodded. "Your dad asked me to pass on a message."

She shuddered, not wanting to think about Dad. Or Mom. "What did he say?"

"He loves you, and he's sorry. He said they did what had to be done to save the town."

She broke down and sobbed, head resting on bended knees, arms wrapped tight around her legs. If Dad loved her, why had he hidden the truth all these years?

———

Joel moved around the picnic table and sat beside Hannah. He placed a comforting hand on her shoulder and quietly prayed. Family relationships were complicated, and no one had perfect parents.

The minutes ticked by, and her racking sobs began to ease. The emotional toll of the last few days had pushed Hannah to breaking point.

He didn't know how to help her. He loved Hannah, and his heart broke seeing her distressed and miserable. How could they fix this situation? What would it mean for their relationship?

She lifted her head and opened her beautiful eyes, red rimmed and puffy. "I'm exhausted."

"My mum reckons a good cry makes her feel better."

Her lips twitched in the direction of a smile. "She sounds like a smart lady."

"She mostly is." Except for the blind spot regarding her husband. Joel couldn't understand why Mum wouldn't push harder to make Mike come home for her knee replacement surgery.

"At least she loves you. My mother ..." She closed her eyes and tipped her head forward.

"You're right about my mum," he said. "She makes mistakes, and can frustrate me, but I know she loves me."

Hannah lifted her head and stared into his eyes, her lower lip wobbling. "I think my mother hates me."

He put his arm around her shoulders, drawing her close in a side hug. "I don't understand your mother."

"That makes two of us."

"And I don't know what to say." He had plenty of thoughts regarding Susannah's behavior, but voicing them now wouldn't be appropriate or helpful.

"Me, either. Maybe I should see a therapist."

"It couldn't hurt." He sensed Hannah had let deep-seated

emotional pain bubble to the surface today. He'd learned it wasn't healthy to lock away negative emotions.

"I don't know what to think. Dad lied to me about the flood zone."

"I'm sorry he did that."

"What bugs me is why he did it."

"Becky said the flood zoning stopped a developer ruining Trinity Lakes."

"That may be true, but Dad could have told me about it on numerous occasions. And he didn't."

"Did you ask him why?"

"He wouldn't answer and told me it didn't matter." Her voice shook and she looked up, meeting his gaze. "But it does matter."

He nodded and pulled her closer. "It doesn't make sense."

"I know, right? If everything was above board, why hide the reasons for the zoning change?"

"It's a mystery." He couldn't shake the idea that Wayne was hiding something.

"Mom made some wild accusations about Dad during their divorce. We didn't know who or what to believe."

"That's hard." Stories about Susannah's bad behavior no longer shocked him.

"Dad promised me back then that he wasn't like Mom. He promised to always tell me the truth."

Hannah's father had broken her trust. He'd also shown genuine remorse and a willingness to take responsibility for his actions. Joel prayed Hannah could talk through the issues with her father and repair their relationship.

She yawned. "I'm so tired."

"Try to rest. I'll hold you and keep you safe."

"Thank you for everything."

"You're welcome." He'd do anything for Hannah.

She snuggled closer, her sweater hood cushioning her cheek

against his chest. He tucked a blanket around her body, creating a warm cocoon.

He stroked her hair, her eyelids flitted closed, and he let out an exhausted breath. *Please, Lord, no more drama today.*

Joel checked his phone, glad he still had a weak signal. Becky had sent him a few updates. Wayne had driven Hannah's SUV to her home. He'd drive his rental to the rowing club to say goodbye to Becky, and he'd likely miss seeing Hannah before he left town for Spokane and the airport.

Joel didn't know if Wayne leaving town was a good or bad thing. Face-to-face conversations to deal with conflict were his preference. Hannah's family operated differently to his own family in how they managed problems and issues.

Becky had canceled her shift at the bakery and stayed at the rowing club to help Tabby. The worst of the storm had passed over the other side of the lake, and they didn't have a leaking roof or structural damage at the rowing club or their homes. A big blessing. Hannah didn't need any more stress.

She looked like she'd fallen into a deep sleep, her shoulders rising and falling in a regular rhythm. The cloud cover shifted, and the sun beamed more warmth through the thinning clouds in the sky.

He kept the bear spray close, his eyes open and alert. They didn't have any food that would attract bears, and he hadn't heard of bears roaming in the area. Adrenaline kept him going, and he'd crash later when Hannah was safe and home in Trinity Lakes.

They'd need to talk about the future of their relationship. Was love enough to overcome the obstacles in their path?

CHAPTER TWELVE

An hour later, a truck pulled into the parking lot near their picnic table. Colombia Search and Rescue. Joel let out a big sigh, his tense muscles starting to unwind. Their wilderness adventure was almost over.

The team of two first responders stepped out of their truck, carrying backpacks packed with supplies, and walked toward him. Hannah was asleep in his lap.

The lady who seemed to be in charge placed her gear on the table and turned to face him. "Hey, I'm Jocelyn, and this is Jesse." She gestured toward the man on her right.

He gave her a weary smile. "I'm Joel, and I'm very glad to see you."

"We bet you are." Jocelyn returned his smile. Her gaze then focused on Hannah. "Is she injured?"

"I don't think so, but she's sleepy."

"Hmm." Her gaze stayed focused on Hannah. "Sorry, you'll need to wake her so we can assess her."

"Okay." Joel brushed loose clumps of muddy hair off her forehead. "Hannah." He whispered in her ear, gently shifting his position on the bench.

The slight jolt of movement stirred her. Hannah stretched and rubbed her knuckles over her eyes. "Where am I?"

"Near the river," Joel said. "The mountain rescue team is here."

"Oh." Hannah sat straighter, appearing to wake quickly.

Jocelyn sat next to Hannah and gave her an encouraging smile as she introduced herself and her partner, who stood by, waiting. "Do you remember what happened and how you ended up here?"

Hannah pressed her lips together and nodded. "I'm sorry. I'm the reason we needed rescuing ..."

"It's no problem," Jocelyn said. "I'm going to do some routine checks and ask you a few more questions. Is that okay?"

"Sure." Worry lines formed between Hannah's eyebrows.

Jocelyn commenced the first aid assessment, including checking Hannah's pulse and shining a small light in each eye. She pulled out a portable blood pressure cuff and blood oxygen level monitor, then recorded all her findings on a tablet.

"Pupils are looking normal." Jocelyn's fingertips tapped the screen. "Hannah, did you injure your head or any other part of your body?"

"No. I dodged the logs in the river."

Joel inhaled a sharp breath. What if one of those logs had hit Hannah?

"Are you experiencing any pain?" Jocelyn asked.

Hannah gave a small nod. "I've had a headache all day, but it's not as bad now."

"Can you stand and walk?"

"I'll try."

Joel removed the blanket and helped her to put on her sneakers.

Hannah stood. She took a few stumbling steps, looking like she'd woken from a long nap.

"I'm fine." Hannah sat beside Joel, her hand seeking his.

He squeezed her hand to reassure her health was looking good.

Jocelyn nodded and switched her attention to Joel. "Do you have any health concerns we should know about?"

"I'm good." He felt a million times better now Hannah had bounced back to something resembling normal.

"Okay." Jocelyn glanced back at her partner before continuing. "At this stage, we won't need to go to the ER. I understand your family and friends are gathered at Trinity Lakes Rowing Club."

Joel nodded. "My truck is there, plus shower facilities."

"You'll want to get cleaned up and check there aren't any open wounds under all the mud." Jocelyn focused on Hannah. "Can someone stay with you overnight? Just in case you've had a bump to the head you don't remember."

"My sister will be there."

"Good. After you clean up, please ask someone to check your scalp for any signs of bruising or bleeding. Keep in mind, concussion symptoms can take a day or two to appear. While everything appears normal right now, your sleepiness could be a symptom of a concussion."

Hannah's eyes widened. "Wouldn't I remember? I don't have amnesia or memory loss."

"It's just a precaution." Jocelyn smiled reassuringly. "Since we're not taking you to the ER. Can you walk to our truck?"

"Yeah, Joel can help me."

Jocelyn winked. "You're lucky to have him with you today."

"I know." Her lips curved into a smile. "He's my hero."

"Aw, you two are cute." Jocelyn smiled.

Hannah's sweet words warmed his heart. Joel hooked his arm around Hannah's waist and helped her walk the short distance to the truck. She chose to sit in the back beside him rather than lie on the stretcher bed.

Joel collected their gear from the picnic table. He pulled on clean socks and a pair of shoes that were one size too big. He appreciated Becky's thoughtfulness.

Jesse secured their kayaks on the truck's roof racks.

Hannah buckled her seat belt and leaned on Joel's shoulder. "I need a nap."

He circled his arm around her shoulders. "We'll be at the rowing club soon."

Her eyelids fluttered closed, and she dropped off to sleep.

Jocelyn frowned, studying Hannah. "Is there a reason she's so tired?"

"We've had a busy and draining couple of days. Do you often attend rescues for Trinity Lakes?"

Jesse climbed into the front driver seat and shut the door. Jocelyn turned toward Joel. "Jesse and I are volunteers with the county search and rescue team. We work rescues throughout the entire county. I'm a paramedic in Trinity Lakes, but today was my day off, so I was able to answer the rescue call."

Jesse glanced back at Joel. "My granddad lives in the hills around here, so whenever I stay with him, I'm on call with the SAR team."

"I'm glad your crew could spare the resources to help us today."

"It's no problem," Jocelyn said. "We usually work with the ski patrol in the winter. Dealing with wildfires and rescuing lost hikers keeps us busy in the off-season."

"In Australia we have our state emergency services, and many of them are volunteers. They help the professionals during floods and bushfires."

Jocelyn nodded. "I've heard Australian wildfires can be bad, much like California."

"It can be scary. Our firefighters are heroes, for sure. They risk their lives to help others."

Jesse swung around in the driver's seat. "Are we ready to roll?"

"Yes." Jocelyn nodded. "Next stop, Trinity Lakes."

Joel sat back in his seat and tucked Hannah's matted hair behind her ear. They both needed showers and clean clothing. He prayed she didn't have a concussion or any other physical injuries. The emotional turmoil of the last few days had taken its toll.

———

HANNAH HELD Joel's hand and stepped out of the rescue truck. The rowing club parking lot was full of vehicles. She joined Joel in thanking both rescuers for their assistance, making a mental note to remember to send the county search and rescue team a generous donation check.

Grandma, then Becky, embraced her in bone-shattering hugs. Their fast spoken words, as they talked over each other, blurred into gobbledygook in her mind. She nodded and pasted on a weak smile, hoping to appease them. Rowing club members wished her well, helping out by retrieving their kayaks and gear from the rescue truck.

She walked toward the clubhouse with Joel, Becky, and Grandma. Her pace was slow, her leg muscles cramping and sore. Joel's firm grip on her hand kept her moving forward.

They reached the clubhouse steps and she leaned against the railing.

Joel smiled and let go of her hand. "I'll organize our gear and clean the kayaks."

"Thanks. I appreciate you," she said.

"Don't worry, Joel," Becky said. "I've raided her office and locker, and everything is ready for her shower."

"Thanks, Becky. I'll head to the changing rooms soon." He climbed the stairs with Grandma and the seniors who had volunteered to help.

Becky stayed by her side, fussing like a crazy hen who'd almost lost all her chicks.

Hannah couldn't wait to wash off the itchy mud and who knew what else from her skin and hair. "What about Joel's clothes?"

"He's good to go. One of his college friends stopped by with clothes and other things he'll need."

"I'm glad." The events from earlier today didn't feel real. After a shower, all she'd want to do was crawl into her warm, cozy bed, and pretend the last few days hadn't happened.

The sun was out, partly obscured by clouds and sitting lower on the western horizon. How many hours had passed? Her stomach grumbled, reminding her she'd need to eat something more substantial than protein bars soon.

Becky cupped her elbow as they walked the long way, up the ramp, to the clubhouse veranda. Hannah held onto the railing, her steps slow. It was more dignified to walk than have Joel carrying her up the steps. He'd already carried her enough times today.

"Tabby went home early," Becky said. "Her family needed her at the inn. We canceled all the afternoon bookings and focused on cleaning up after the storm."

"Is there any damage?"

"No, thankfully. Only a few tree branches fell, missing the buildings and cars in the lot. The campground and RV park are fine, but there was minor flooding in the campground from the heavy downpour and a blocked drainpipe. It's cleared now. We were fortunate."

Hannah nodded. Fortunate was an understatement. Her life, and Joel's life, had been spared. How different things could have turned out if she'd not acted quickly to reach the riverbank … although the whole situation could have been avoided if she'd stopped to think first, rather than impulsively making dumb decisions.

Joel walked over to her side. He was covered in mud and looked exhausted. "The seniors are taking care of the kayaks. I'll clean up now, then drive you home. Can we talk later?"

"Okay." She closed her eyes for a moment, gathering her thoughts. "I'm tired and might not feel up to talking."

He pressed his lips together, looking like he had a lot to say, but holding back. "Sure. Rest is important."

She reached for his hand, clasping it within hers. "Thanks for everything."

He held her gaze, his eyes soft and smile sweet. "We can talk when you're ready. There's no rush."

Her heart warmed at the kindness and care in his tone and words. She loved him, and she couldn't put into words how much his sacrificial love meant to her. He'd put his own life at risk to save hers.

Joel was one of a kind, a rare gem she'd thought she'd never find this side of heaven. She prayed they could overcome this storm and plan a future together.

Hannah took her time showering, then changed into the nice-smelling, warm clothes Becky had provided. Her damp hair no longer exuded swamp scent, and the skin itch had eased. Becky had checked Hannah's scalp, and Hannah had been relieved when Becky said it looked fine. No need for a trip to the ER.

The clubhouse was quieter, with most of their loyal senior members leaving once they'd helped pack up for the day. Their cleaner had arrived early for her usual shift, and she'd finish soon, thanks to a few of the seniors who'd chipped in to help. More volunteers were needed in other parts of town that hadn't fared as well in the storm.

Grandma had a steaming cup of tea waiting for Hannah. "This will make you feel better, my dear girl."

"Thanks." She sipped the soothing chamomile tea, glad to be back in Trinity Lakes.

Joel pulled up a chair beside her and thanked Grandma for his tea. He looked Hannah straight in the eye. "How are you feeling, honestly? Is your headache gone?"

"Almost gone." She held the warm mug between her hands.

"Hello." The high-pitched voice silenced the room.

Hannah cringed, recognizing Mom's voice and footsteps behind her. She couldn't. She just couldn't. She didn't have the energy to go another round with Mom, not after everything that had happened today.

"Darling, my poor sweetheart, are you okay?" Mom's saccharine tone had rolled into overdrive. No doubt an audience of curious seniors lingering nearby incentivized her need to impress.

She avoided Mom's gaze, her grip tightening on her mug. "I'm fine."

"I was so worried." Mom passed a large picnic hamper to Joel. "When I heard you two were on your way here, I stopped by Leah's store and picked up Hannah's favorites for your dinner tonight."

Joel's eyes widened. "Thank you, but you didn't need to—"

"Of course I needed to buy your dinner. You risked your life to save my daughter."

"Thanks for dinner, but Mom, I thought you and Joel—"

Mom raised her palm in the universal stop sign position. "Joel is the hero of the day." Mom turned to the handful of people observing their conversation, her voice loud. "Don't you all think Joel deserves a round of applause."

Everyone started clapping and cheering, and Joel's face reddened. Talk about uncomfortable.

"Okay." Hannah addressed the room. "Thank you all for your help today. We appreciate you, too."

Mom narrowed her eyes, her goodwill switching into shutdown mode. "I must go. Hannah, I'll be out of town for the next few days. Grandma can help if you need anything."

"Mom, about yesterday, at your party. The conversation between you and Joel—"

"Hannah, I don't know what you're talking about. My party was fabulous, and everyone had a great time. There's nothing to discuss. Nothing of importance. Goodbye." Mom spun on her heel, strode toward Grandma, air-kissed Grandma's cheek, and left the clubhouse.

Joel's mouth gaped. "What just happened?"

"Mom is moody." Why had she expected anything different, especially when they had an audience?

He drank his tea, and his mouth curved into a frown. "What she said to me, about us, at her party. She acted like it never happened."

She nodded. "Mom does this all the time. She changes the subject and won't acknowledge or address problems."

His frown deepened. "I guess we can talk at dinner, when we won't be overheard."

"A good plan. Once the cleaning is done, Becky can help us lock up."

"That works for me," he said.

Hannah finished her tea, then it was time to leave. She was quiet during the short drive to her home in Joel's truck, her mind preoccupied by the drama of the last few days.

Mom's behavior at the clubhouse was the pinnacle of everything Hannah hated. Why couldn't Mom have an adult conversation and work on finding a compromise? If Mom didn't get her way, she either threw a tantrum or used the silent treatment. Mom acting like something hadn't happened drove Hannah nuts.

Joel unpacked the hamper on Hannah's kitchen island. "Veggie lasagna, chicken cobb salad, spinach salad, and garlic bread. I can't fault your mother's taste in food, and it was kind of her to provide dinner."

She nodded. Kindness with a catch. When Mom randomly

did something nice, the action was usually followed by a nasty sting. What was she up to this time?

He placed the salad containers in the fridge. "I'll put the lasagna in the oven, and I'll add the garlic bread soon."

"Thanks. An early dinner sounds great. I'm hungry."

"That's not surprising." He joined her at the kitchen island, pulling out a stool to sit beside her. "I'd like to share something with you."

"Sure. What's it about?"

"My ex in Sydney, and the circumstances of our split."

"Oh …"

He reached for her hand, threading his fingers through hers. "She blindsided me by the way she broke off our relationship. She wouldn't tell me why, other than saying it was about her, not me."

Hannah swallowed the lump building in her throat. "That's a bit rough. Saying it's over and not telling you why."

"I took it hard." He rubbed his hand behind his neck, his face tense, and eyes distant. "She said she loved me, but it wasn't enough."

"That hurts." When was love not enough? She empathized with the harsh sting of rejection.

"She also said she couldn't be the wife I deserved."

Hannah closed her eyes for a moment, feeling the intensity of his pain in her heart. "I'm sorry she hurt you. It must have been horrible."

He nodded. "Those were dark days. My family, Zach, Billie, and other friends rallied around me."

"I'm glad you had support." She never underestimated the blessing of supportive family and friends.

"I needed it. The rumor mill at church went crazy, and I was blamed for the breakup."

She shook her head. "That's hard and unfair."

"Yeah." He paused, as if he was searching for the right words.

"I couldn't say anything to shut down the gossip because I wanted to protect her privacy."

"You're a good man, Joel. Many people would have thrown her under the bus."

"That's not who I am. I stayed quiet, and three months later she requested a meeting."

"Really? She needed closure, or something?" Many people would move on, never looking back at the trail of destruction left behind. Or they were like her mother and pretended the destruction didn't exist.

"Not exactly. But our meeting gave me closure and some answers. She said she'd been in therapy and shared how she'd experienced a traumatic situation a decade earlier that she'd buried and tried to ignore."

She covered her mouth with her hand. "Oh no, that poor girl. And you had no clue?"

He shook his head. "When we started talking about engagements and marriage, her trauma wouldn't stay buried, and she couldn't handle it." He stared into her eyes, holding her gaze. "She broke up with me and continued unpacking a whole lot of emotional stuff in therapy."

Hannah rested her elbow on the kitchen island, feeling the weight of Joel's words. She had emotional stuff to unpack, too. "It must have been difficult for her to share this with you."

"It was." He shifted his gaze to the window, looking lost in the memories. "I didn't want or need to know the details. It's her private business."

She nodded. Joel hadn't shared his ex's name, and she wasn't going to ask.

"She shared enough to explain her decision to do mission work."

"That's helpful." The poor girl had helped Joel move on. A brave decision. "I'm guessing she wanted time and space to heal in a different environment."

"Yes." He glanced at the timer he'd set for the lasagna on his phone.

Hannah sat straighter on the stool and stretched out her legs. "It sounds like she's on a journey to healing."

"She said it was a long-term process. She wanted to focus on strengthening her relationship with Jesus."

Hannah traced her thumb over his fingertips, appreciating his honesty. She was thankful Joel trusted her enough to have this conversation. "I'm glad the traumatic experience didn't cause her to lose her faith."

"Me, too. She acknowledged our relationship had helped her to take steps to deal with past hurts."

"That sounds like a positive outcome." Her stomach growled. She eyed the garlic bread on a nearby tray, ready to go in the oven.

"It was a steep learning curve for me, too." He leaned closer and tucked loose strands of hair behind her ear, his fingertips skimming her cheek. "I learned the importance of extending grace when we don't know what's going on with the other person. Sometimes we can't know the reasons or circumstances why people choose to make certain decisions."

Hannah closed her eyes for a few seconds, trying to ignore her hunger pangs and collect her thoughts. "I know I need to forgive Dad for not telling me about the secret land deal."

"Forgiveness benefits us more than the other person. Holding onto grudges and unforgiveness is soul-destroying."

"That's true. Mom can't let go of grudges, and she's miserable."

He nodded. "One reason I decided to travel was to press the reset button, and not continue being defined by a past relationship."

"Understandable." It was unfair that people had judged Joel.

His phone alarm chimed, and he stood. He ducked around the island and slid the garlic bread into the oven.

Rich lasagna flavors escaped the hot oven and filled her senses. She couldn't wait to eat.

He stood across from her, his expression caring and serious. "Your father loves you, Hannah, and he's sorry. He never wanted to hurt you."

She pursed her lips, processing the truth in his words. "I didn't handle his secret reveal well. Mom had pushed me to my limit, and his betrayal tipped me over. I assumed there must be a bad reason for hiding the land deal."

"Here's the thing. What we do know is the town got the right outcome. The town you love wasn't destroyed by a crazy hotel and mall monstrosity."

"Yeah, but I'm still stuck on the why. If Dad had nothing to hide, why didn't he say something earlier?" That was the question she couldn't get out of her mind.

"You'll have to ask him. At least you know he had a noble reason for doing what he did."

"I guess so." She wanted to understand why, and only Dad could give her the answer. "Dad sent me a text. He said he'll call me early tomorrow morning, when he lands in Florida."

"A good night's sleep will help you clarify your thoughts."

"I hope so." Joel was right. The end goal of stopping the developer from ruining the town was noble. If the same situation took place now, she'd do everything possible to avoid selling her land to a developer.

Had Dad done something dodgy to prevent the developer from buying the land? She couldn't fault his recent handling of her trust fund, and she knew he had her best interests at heart. She may need to accept that she may never learn the truth.

———

JOEL SWALLOWED his last mouthful of lasagna and contemplated a second serving. Leah's delicious fresh food never failed to exceed his expectations. Unlike real life, which had its share of disappointments. He'd been stunned a few hours earlier when Susannah had given them the dinner hamper and created a happy family scene in the rowing club.

Had Susannah wanted to pretend she'd said nothing at her party, and everything was fine? Or was her act of kindness a performance for the benefit of the seniors? He couldn't figure it out.

Hannah smiled from across the table. "This is good. Leah's lasagna is the best."

"It really is." He refilled his glass of sparkling water, eyeing the leftover lasagna. Another serving of salad would be healthier. The garlic bread, which they'd already finished, had been amazing.

Hannah scooped more spinach salad on her plate, her pretty smile lingering on her relaxed face. Eating great food seemed to have given her a burst of energy.

His phone rang and he glanced at the screen. Mum. Why was she calling?

"Please take the call," Hannah said.

"Okay." He stood and answered the call, walking away from the table. "Hey, Mum, what's up?"

"Can we talk without anyone overhearing?"

"Sure." He pointed to the door to the hallway, and Hannah nodded. He headed along the hall toward Hannah's spacious living room. Becky had earlier walked to Gracie's home for a discreet dinner without Susannah. Hannah's sister had shared with Joel her absolute frustration and disgust with her mother's behavior.

"Okay Mum, I'm on my own. What's going on?"

"It's Bella. She's at North Sydney Police Station."

"She's what?" He checked the time and did the math. It was mid-morning in Sydney. "Isn't she supposed to be in school?"

"Yeah, she ditched school to go joyriding with her boyfriend in a stolen Lamborghini that he crashed into a power pole."

"What the what? Has she been arrested?"

"They're still discussing whether or not charges will be laid. Apparently the boyfriend is related to the owner of the car and somehow got hold of the keys."

He closed his eyes. "Oh boy. What a mess."

"Yeah. Thankfully the car crashed at low speed, and they weren't injured."

Thank you, Jesus. Bella was okay. A big relief. "How did it happen?" Did he want to know?

"She said a cat ran on the road. They hit the curb and the pole to avoid the cat."

He shook his head, picturing Mum's words in his mind. "So they weren't speeding?"

"Not when the accident happened." Mum paused. "But the police tracked the car via different cameras in the city, and they were traveling over the speed limit in the tunnels and on other roads."

"I can't believe she did this." Bella loved fast cars, and she was the kid who'd tagged along with her father to car shows and car racing events. "What else do you know?"

"It's not good news. Bella claims she didn't know the luxury car was stolen because the boyfriend had the keys. He did have a valid driver's license."

"That's a good thing, I guess. Do the police believe her story?" Did he believe Bella was telling the truth? The temptation to ride in a Lamborghini was too big for his sister to resist.

"I honestly don't know. I'm sitting in a cafe drinking coffee and wondering where I went wrong as a parent. What am I going to do with her?"

"You'll think of something."

"I'm out of answers, and her father is disengaged. He doesn't want to know."

"What's going on with him, and why isn't he home with you in Sydney?"

Mum paused. "I was hoping to keep this under wraps, but I think you deserve the truth. Mike and I have been having relationship problems for a while. The New Zealand job was a trial separation, to see if some time apart could help us. Last weekend, we decided to split for good."

"Oh Mum, I'm sorry. I had wondered if something was wrong, and I'm sad for you all. How are Bella and Jack taking the news?"

Mum sniffed, and sounded like she might be crying. "We haven't told them. There's enough drama going on, between Bella's antics and my knee surgery."

"You can't hide this from them forever. They deserve to hear the truth, too."

"I know. Can you come home and help me? Please …"

The parental heartstrings pulled tight, threatening to choke him. Mum wasn't exaggerating the situation. Bella was in serious trouble, but she might listen to him.

"Joel, you don't have to answer right now. I'll call you back in a few hours when I know more about Bella's situation, and if she needs a lawyer."

"Okay. I'll need to see what I can juggle here. Summer camp starts mid-June and—"

"I can pay for your airfares and expenses and have you back in the States in time for summer camp. I know this is a major inconvenience, and I feel bad that I'm asking you to come home."

He rubbed his hand through his hair. "We'll work it out. I need to go and talk to a few people."

"Sure. I love you, irrespective of your decision. If you can come home, that would be a big help. Chat later."

The line went dead, and Joel closed his eyes.

Lord, what do I do? I feel like going home to help Mum's the right decision, but maybe it isn't?

He made his way back to Hannah. She'd cleared the table and was packing the dishwasher.

"Is everything okay in Australia?" she asked.

He shook his head. "Just when you think today can't get any worse, tomorrow in Australia starts off with a disaster. Bella was arrested in a stolen car after it crashed into a power pole."

Her mouth fell open. "How did that happen?"

"Poor judgment and the irresistible lure of a Lamborghini." He shared his sister's tale of woe with Hannah.

"Wow. Do you think she's telling the truth?"

"I hope so. The car being owned by his family gives her story more credibility. But that's not all. Mum had more bad news."

"No, really? What else could go wrong?"

"Mum and Mike have separated, and it doesn't look like they'll reconcile."

"Oh Joel, I'm sorry." She walked around the island and embraced him in a warm hug. "What does this mean?"

He lifted her chin, holding her gaze. "I think I'll be catching a plane home to Australia ASAP."

Her lower lip trembled. "You're leaving."

"My family needs me. I need to call my boss and give Mum an answer this evening."

"What about us?" Her voice was unsteady, her tone communicating her concern.

"We need to talk about our future and work out a plan before I fly out."

She looked up and nodded. "You better go and make arrangements."

He dropped a kiss on her soft lips, wishing he could stay in her arms longer. But duty called. "We can work this out, if that's what you want."

"I can't pack up and go to Australia with you this week, if that's what you're asking."

He shook his head. "I wouldn't ask you to do that. But if we are to have a future together, we need to work out which country we'd choose." Australia or the USA. A tough decision. Could he settle down with Hannah in Trinity Lakes, knowing her mother despised him?

CHAPTER THIRTEEN

Hannah poured hot water from her kettle into a mug at her kitchen island and jiggled the green tea bag. It was six in the morning, and Dad would be video calling her any minute. She'd tossed and turned all night, her mind preoccupied by everything that had happened yesterday. Joel would be leaving Trinity Lakes tomorrow for Spokane Airport, and that news had rocked her world.

Joel had spoken to his mother last night, and she'd booked him a one-way ticket home. He'd fly into Sydney on Friday morning, the same day his mother's knee surgery was scheduled. He hadn't confirmed when he planned to return to Trinity Lakes. Bella had escaped being charged, although she'd received a stern warning from the police to stay out of trouble.

The video call flashed on her phone screen, and she accepted the call. Her father's tired face appeared. It didn't look like he'd slept any better than her on his red-eye flight home.

"Hannah, I appreciate you waking early to talk."

"It's okay. I didn't sleep well after all the drama yesterday." She filled Dad in on Joel's family situation and his impending departure.

"I'm sorry, honey. That's a hard situation. It sounds like his family needs him right now."

"Yeah, I know. I can understand why he's leaving."

"Have you two talked about your future? It's obvious to me that you both have feelings for each other, but I'm also aware your mother is causing problems."

"We're catching up this afternoon at the rowing club after I finish work." She cradled her warm cup of tea in her hands. "I'm not sure if he wants to take on the baggage of my family. We live on different sides of the world."

"That's just geography," Dad said. "We live in a global village, and we can stay connected via technology. It's not like you don't have the money to travel overseas and visit family."

"I'm worried Mom has scared him off. She's been horrible to him, and I don't know what I can do …"

"Have you prayed? Asked the big guy upstairs to help you work it out?"

Dad was talking about praying? The world was topsy-turvy today. She lifted her cup to her lips, his words brewing in her mind as she drank her tea. "I'm praying and seeking wisdom."

"Good. I have faith you'll work out a solution with Joel." Dad adjusted his glasses and smoothed over his thinning gray hair. "I want to talk to you about the land deal."

"I'm listening." She'd try to keep an open mind and give Dad the benefit of the doubt. Innocent until proven guilty.

"I made mistakes back then. I got the right result and saved the town, but I'm not proud of how we got the result. I've tried over the years to take care of the people who were involved, to make amends."

"Who are these people?"

"I'm sorry, but I can't tell you. It's not my story to share. If I had my time over, I'd have made different decisions. But what's done is done, and I can't change the past."

Hannah sipped her tea, pondering his words. "So you regret what took place."

"You have no idea how many regrets I have over that flood zoning situation. Being mayor at the time, I felt like I had the responsibility of the whole town on my shoulders. It was a difficult situation to fix, and I didn't want to fail the good people of Trinity Lakes."

"Just to clarify that I have this clear in my mind." She took her time, piecing together the bits of information he'd provided. "You were in a tight corner and made the wrong choices. And you live with the consequences, more than two decades later."

"That pretty much sums it up. People got hurt, and I've carried the guilt. Can you understand why I didn't want to talk about it and dredge up the past?"

She nodded. "I appreciate you telling me your story. I'm sorry I reacted badly and took off kayaking. That was my dumb decision."

"At lunch, I didn't know how much pressure your mother had put on you. Little wonder you had a headache. When Becky told me what had happened, I called your mother and made it very clear that her behavior toward Joel was unacceptable."

She pushed her empty cup aside and leaned forward on her elbows, concentrating on the screen. "That explains why Mom randomly turned up at the rowing club with a dinner basket from Leah's store."

"Did she apologize to Joel?"

"Of course not. She acted like nothing had happened."

"Sweetheart, please don't be fooled by what looks like your mother's act of kindness." He took off his glasses, revealing dark shadows around his eyes. "During our phone call—that included a lot of shouting and yelling and name calling—your mother made it clear she's unrepentant. She wants you to break up with Joel."

Her heart sank like a boulder tumbling into a lake. Mom

hated Joel. Dad's words played over in her mind. "Mom was yelling and rude to you. Seriously?"

He rubbed his hand over his face. "That's normal for her."

"I had no idea …" Dad had never said anything, although she shouldn't be surprised. It was no different to how Mom had behaved back when Dad filed for divorce.

"Phone calls with your mother are never pleasant. She'll never forgive me for leaving her. And she always brings up the past and my so-called list of sins of how I've wronged her."

"I'm sorry you have to deal with that."

He shifted position, looking like he was uncomfortable in his seat. "It is what it is, and it's her problem that she holds grudges forever."

"I'm thinking about getting therapy. It couldn't hurt."

He smiled. "Been there, done that, and I highly recommend it."

She widened her eyes. Dad was full of surprises today. "I'll definitely look into it."

"I love you, Hannah. I want you to be happy. Don't let your mother control your life or steal your joy."

"Okay, Dad. I love you, too."

"I'd better let you go and get ready for work. Send my regards to Joel and pass on my thanks to him for rescuing you yesterday. He's a keeper, Hannah. Don't forget that."

"I won't, Dad. Bye." She shut down the call and blotted the tears threatening to flow. Dad was right. Joel was worth fighting for, and she trusted that God would provide a path to bring them together in His timing.

She pulled herself together and got ready to leave for work. Being busy at the rowing club would help pass the time and let her think about her conversation with Dad.

Her morning at work flew by. She'd had a lot to do, since she'd left early yesterday. Grandma had stopped by with her regular morning latte and words of encouragement. During their conversation, Grandma had let her know she'd had a conversation with Mom regarding the way she was treating Joel. Mom had tried to deny she'd said anything mean to Joel, and Grandma had told Mom to stay out of Hannah's business. That conversation had taken place after Mom dropped off Hannah's dinner.

Becky arrived on time with leftover pastries to share for lunch. They settled outside at a table where they'd have privacy to talk.

Hannah chose a mini quiche. "Did Grandma tell you she spoke with Mom about Joel?"

Becky nodded. "We talked about Mom at dinner. I'm so over dealing with all the gaslighting."

"What do you mean? What's gaslighting?"

"It's when Mom says or does something, and then later pretends it never happened. When you try to bring up the subject, she brushes you off and acts like you're making up stories. Then she tells you what happened isn't the truth."

"Oh." Hannah reached for her water bottle. "Dad thinks it's a good idea to do therapy."

"You've spoken to him today."

"This morning." Hannah filled Becky in on the details.

"I need comfort food." Becky chose a chocolate croissant and took a bite. "Your instincts were right about the land deal. Are you going to tell Tabby?"

Hannah shook her head. "I don't know anything new, and what happened is in the past. My understanding is Tabby's family can apply for a zoning change, and it should go through without any issues."

"Will that impact the zoning of your land?"

"I'm not sure. That's a problem for another day."

"Agreed." Becky finished her croissant. "You're meeting Joel this afternoon, right?"

"After work. It's a beautiful day for a walk along the lake."

"Please don't let Mom stop you from pursuing a relationship with Joel."

Hannah curved her mouth into a wide smile. "You're the third person to say that to me today."

"The three of us want you to be happy." Becky grinned like a cat who'd consumed a gallon of cream. "If Dad and Grandma and me are all in agreement, we must be right."

She flicked her hair back over her shoulders. "I know I need to overcome my fears and trust God to work out the details."

"I'll be praying," Becky said.

"I'm blessed to have you as my sister."

"Backatcha. I'll always have your back."

Hannah could benefit from a large dose of Becky's optimism. She should be dwelling on positive things instead of wallowing in negativity. Mom may remain an unresolved problem, but she could take steps and learn how to manage their relationship. It was time to stop living in fear and embrace the future possibilities with Joel. She'd count the minutes until she'd see him this afternoon.

———

AT LUNCHTIME ON TUESDAY, Joel parked his truck under a tree by the river and called his father. They'd lined up the call last night, and his father had woken at five in the morning to squeeze in the phone call.

Joel switched his phone to loudspeaker mode. "Morning, Dad."

"Good afternoon to you. How's yesterday treating you?"

He chuckled. "Much better than the day before. I have a few things to tell you." Joel shared the details of his conversations with Mum.

Dad let out a low whistle. "So Bella would rather cruise

around Sydney in a Lamborghini than go to school. Can't say I blame her."

"Dad! She's only fourteen and should be getting an education."

"I know, and I hope she took the warning from the police seriously."

"I'll soon find out. Can you fit in a trip to Sydney in the next few weeks?"

"Absolutely. I'm sorry about the circumstances with your mother, but it will be good to see you."

"She's not having an easy time."

"It sounds like she's been a single parent for a while."

"Yeah, I had wondered if the New Zealand job was a separation. She's taking the breakup hard." Maybe he should have asked Mum more questions about the state of her marriage. But Mum had been denying that Mike's decision to live in Auckland was due to marital issues for months.

"Is Mike keeping in touch with his kids?" Dad asked.

"I'm a bit hazy on the details. Mum said he was disengaged, which doesn't sound good."

"She did a great job in raising you, and she'll keep on loving those kids through to adulthood."

"True. I'm only now appreciating how good it was that you and Mum co-parented and somehow remained on friendly terms. I never felt like I was in the middle of your disagreements."

"Our marriage may have failed, but we were determined to prioritize your wellbeing. Your mother and I didn't hold grudges, and we left the past in the past. I was happy when she remarried, and I'm sad to hear her marriage is in trouble. I'll be praying for you all, and especially for Bella and Jack to have their father more involved in their lives."

"We appreciate all your prayers. Mum has asked me to pray

for her a few times. I'm praying that's a sign she's turning to Jesus and relying on her faith to give her strength."

"We're all on a journey. Some of us stray off the narrow path and get caught in the weeds, and it takes us longer to find our way back."

He nodded. "That narrow path is easy to stray from."

"Life isn't easy, son, and sometimes we don't realize we're making unwise decisions until much later."

"I'm meeting Hannah this afternoon to talk about our future. I'll admit I'm struggling with her mother. I can't make sense of her behavior."

"Don't forget your relationship is with Hannah, and not her mother. It's Hannah's job to manage her relationship with her family."

He stared at the river. Calm and peaceful water ebbed and flowed along the banks. He wanted peace in his life. "I love Hannah, but how can I consider a more serious relationship if her mother hates me?"

"You don't have to stay in Trinity Lakes. Plenty of couples intentionally move away from their families for a range of reasons. You could even move to Australia and live on the other side of the world, thousands of miles away from Hannah's mother. Those verses in Genesis talk about leaving your parents for a reason."

He wriggled in his seat, switching to a more comfortable position. "A part of me feels like I'm failing Hannah. What if she chooses her mother over me?"

"That's a valid concern, and something to discuss with Hannah. From what you've said, Hannah's mother sounds like a troubled person with a long history of broken relationships. Hannah's mother is the problem person, and it's up to Hannah to decide where her priorities lie."

"That makes sense. The rest of the family support our relationship, including her father."

"Which proves my point—you're not the problem. Relationships can be hard work, and it sounds like Hannah is worth the effort."

"Thanks, Dad. I'm feeling more confident now."

"I'm glad. Tell Hannah how you feel and what you're looking for in a relationship. I know the circumstances of your last relationship has left you a little gun-shy, but if you love Hannah, you have nothing to lose and everything to gain in telling her you love her."

"Okay Dad, I'll call you later."

"I'll be praying. Love you, son."

"Love you, Dad." Joel ended the call with a smile on his face. He loved Hannah, and he'd follow his father's wise advice. He looked forward to seeing her soon.

———

A FEW HOURS LATER, Hannah waited for Joel at a picnic table outside the rowing club. He walked around the corner from the parking lot, and she met him on the lakeside path. She circled her arms around his waist and buried her face against his chest. His rhythmic heartbeat soothed and calmed her frazzled nerves. They could make this work.

He tipped up her chin and dropped a sweet kiss on her welcoming lips. "It's so good to see you."

"I can't believe you'll be gone tomorrow."

"It doesn't seem real yet. Can we walk and talk?"

"Sure." She held his hand, her fingers entwined with his. "Which direction?"

"Let's head toward town. We can stop somewhere for afternoon tea—maybe the Bellbird."

"Okay." She fell into step beside him.

Had it only been three months since she'd first met Joel on the rowing club veranda, and been intrigued by the charming

Aussie with the gorgeous accent who'd now won her heart? Photos and videos in her phone tracked the progress of their friendship turning into something more.

Lord, please help us find the middle ground and discover how we can make our relationship work in the longer term.

She lengthened her stride to keep up with his pace. "I'm going to miss our afternoon tea breaks. And hitting the water to row or kayak."

"It's not great timing. Now the weather is warmer, I'll be missing out on the longer days and mild breezes."

"Is your return flight booked?"

He shook his head. "I'm leaving the date open in case I can return sooner. I'll definitely be back in time for summer camp in mid-June."

"Yay." His words gave her hope. "You won't be in Australia for long."

"A month away from you will feel like a long time."

"Tell me about it." They passed the sailing club, and she waved hello to the members congregating at the dock. "How's everything going with your mother and Bella?"

"Somehow Bella is one hundred percent off the hook regarding the car theft situation."

"That's great news. I mean, as long as she's learning from her mistakes."

"Mum's hoping Bella will settle down and start making better choices."

A family of swans floated along on the current beside them. The fluffy white cygnets were cute. "Did the boyfriend's family drop the charges?"

"They sure did, mostly to keep the story out of the media. Being under eighteen, the media can't legally publish their names. The boyfriend's uncle, who owns the Lamborghini, is a high-profile person who didn't want any bad press."

"Understandable. What about the damage to the car?"

"Apparently the Lamborghini dashcam footage verified their cat story was true."

"I knew it." The cat story had sounded plausible. Mischief had no traffic sense and needed supervision any time Becky let her outdoors. "I'm glad Bella told the truth."

"Yeah, it made Mum feel a bit better. The speeding fines led to the boyfriend losing a chunk of cash and his license. But here's the twist in the story—the uncle is a cat person, and he didn't have a problem with paying for the damage because they saved the cat."

"Oh, wow, Bella was lucky."

"It's an answer to prayer, assuming she's learned her lesson."

"It sure is. I can sort of understand why she cut school to cruise in a Lamborghini. Leanna is impulsive enough to do that, too."

"Yeah, my dad had the same thought. Mum's calming down, thankfully, and she's making progress in negotiating and reasoning with Bella."

"That's good news, and you'll be there to help her at home after her surgery."

He chuckled. "I'm going to call myself the taxi driver. Bella and Jack's schedule is full-on, with sports and other activities. Mum wouldn't have time to work a day job."

"Will she need to work, if the separation is permanent?"

"Probably not. Mike has always been a generous guy, and money isn't something she worries about."

"That's good. I had a constructive conversation with Dad this morning, before work."

"He got home early."

"Dad made the video call when he collected his car from the airport in Florida." She gave him a short recap of their conversation.

"Are you really okay with what went down all those years ago?" he asked.

She nodded. "I'm sad that people were hurt, but I've accepted that Dad did what he thought was best at the time."

"Hindsight would come in handy. We can't predict the future."

"Yeah, and Tabby knows the flood zoning can be reviewed at any time."

"Did she ask questions?"

"Surprisingly, no. She's preoccupied with stuff that's happening in her life, and she's happy that the zoning change is possible." Hannah was thankful Tabby didn't know about her father's involvement. They could all forget about the past and move on.

"Fair enough. You have plenty of family problems with your mother."

"Ain't that the truth." She squeezed his hand and quickened her pace. Walking at Joel's speed was almost the equivalent of jogging.

How could she prevent Mom from interfering and ruining her relationship with Joel? She'd heeded Dad's advice and accepted that Mom didn't have Hannah's best interests at heart regarding Joel. A bitter and poisonous pill to swallow and try to process.

They walked in silence, the stone bridge in town becoming closer with each step.

Joel slowed his pace, his head turned toward the lake. "What's the Junk Man doing in the water?"

Hannah followed Joel's gaze. The Junk Man was knee-deep in the lake, bending over. It looked like he was examining a small bird. "I recently learned from Becky that the Junk Man tries to help injured wildlife."

"That explains it. I've heard people talking about the Junk Man, but they never mentioned he cared for the birds."

She quickened her pace, looking away from the Junk Man as they passed by on the walking path. "I don't know how Becky found out. I guess she talks to a lot of people when making their coffee."

"She is easy to talk to, and she keeps their secrets."

"I'm glad my sisters don't gossip. Mom, on the other hand …"

"Hannah, we need to talk about your mother. Today. Before I leave Trinity Lakes."

She groaned. "I don't want to think about her. She's toxic."

"Which is why we can't bury our heads in the sand and pretend she won't cause more problems."

"Yeah, I know." Why did real life have to be so hard, so painful? Her wounded heart was scarred and battered by Mom's bitterness and inability to compromise.

They walked under the stone bridge and followed the path along the river. Joel led her to the park bench where they'd shared their first kiss. What a beautiful day. She'd cherish the memories and hold them close to her heart.

She sat on the bench and shifted to face him. "Joel, I don't know what I can do about Mom other than run away and move to Australia."

He laughed and reached for her hand. "Australia is definitely an option, but a move that big would need to be made for the right reasons."

He had a point. Running away wouldn't fix anything, and the problems at home would remain. Home. Could she leave Trinity Lakes and find a new home in Australia?

She searched his eyes, seeking answers. "Do you want me to move to Australia?"

His blue eyes widened a fraction. "I want you to be happy." He tucked loose strands of hair behind her ear. "If that means I stay in Trinity Lakes, I can make that work."

She let out a sharp gasp, and her lungs forgot to breathe. Did she hear him right? She drew in a ragged breath, full of hope and expectation. "You'd move to Trinity Lakes, for me."

His smile could light up all the dark shadows under the stone bridge. "I love you, Hannah Gilbertson. For better or worse, I'd like the privilege of being an important part of your life."

"I love you, too, Joel Manning. I want to make us work."

He lowered his head. She welcomed his kiss, her arms holding him close, her lips showing him how much she cared. The sweet kiss was heady and intoxicating, and the problems they faced faded to gray then faded away, morphing into the vibrant colors of a cloudy sunrise. A new day, a new start, and a new beginning with the man she loved. She could stay in his arms forever.

He lifted his head. "As much as I'd love to spend all afternoon kissing, we have decisions to make."

The clock was ticking, and he'd be leaving Trinity Lakes in less than twenty-four hours.

She inhaled a big breath and a boatload of courage. "I'll be praying I can break free and distance myself from Mom's influence. I can see how her unsupportive behavior will be damaging if I don't set strong boundaries."

He nodded. "Appropriate boundaries are so important. And I'm relieved you can see why you need to prioritize your health and well-being."

"I've discovered I can do therapy online, through video calls. I don't want to see anyone close to home and risk Mom somehow finding out."

"I think the less she knows about your life—and about us—the better."

"Do you really think we can co-exist in the same small town as Mom?"

"I think God is bigger than all the chaos and pain that circulates in your mother's world. If He wants us to live in Trinity Lakes, I trust that He will find a way for us to thrive despite your mother living up the road."

She nodded. "Why do I put Jesus in a box, and forget that if he can conquer death, and bear the punishment for our sins, then He can protect us from my mother's nasty venom?"

"It's called being human. We aren't perfect, and we'll keep on making mistakes, but if we're willing to repent and forgive and not hold grudges, we can overcome the obstacles your mother, other people, and circumstances will throw in our path."

Repent and forgive. She smiled and hugged Joel close, thankful they had options for a wonderful future together. Then the reality of tomorrow hit. She blinked, the tears building and threatening to spill. A month apart would be hard, but it would be a sweet reunion when Joel returned to Trinity Lakes in June. Saying goodbye was tough, but she couldn't wait to see him again.

CHAPTER FOURTEEN

Hannah leaned back in an outdoor chair on her deck and stared at the pretty twilight view of Trinity Lakes and the mountains. It was a warm summer evening, and the citronella candles on her wooden table repelled the bugs.

Joel manned the outdoor grill for their Fourth of July celebration dinner. He'd returned from Australia in early June and had enjoyed volunteering at summer camp. He'd be leaving Trinity Lakes with his friends from college next week, embarking on their road trip to the east coast via the Great Lakes and Niagara Falls.

A few of the competent and hard-working older teens who she'd employed had the potential to take on a larger supervisory role, but the rowing club was too busy for Hannah to take vacation time. Still, with their help, she could consider scheduling more time away from work.

Joel grinned and placed a platter of grilled salmon filets on the table. "Dinner is served."

An appreciative smile curved her lips. "Thank you. It looks and smells divine." She uncovered the salads and crusty French bread rolls. Salmon was her favorite, and she was glad Joel liked it, too.

He reached for her hand. She closed her eyes, appreciating his prayer and blessing of their meal. Becky was out tonight with friends, and Hannah finally had alone time with Joel where they could eat and relax and enjoy each other's company.

She sliced her salmon and took a bite. Delicious, as usual.

Mischief let out a loud and mournful meow from inside the screen door. The cat wasn't allowed out at night, and she wasn't shy in reminding Hannah how unfair they were to keep her indoors.

She turned in her chair, giving Mischief a stern look. "No. You've already had your dinner."

The cat stretched up on her hind legs, dug her front paws into the mesh screen, and amplified her insistent meowing.

"I'm ignoring her." She turned to Joel. "She'll eventually quit complaining."

"I hope so. Are her claws okay?" He pointed to the tips of Mischief's claws which poked through the screen.

She nodded. "I installed expensive cat friendly screens a few years ago, after Mischief shredded the original screen."

"A smart move." Joel chucked. "If Becky moves out, does that mean Mischief leaves too?"

"It sure does. That cat is Becky's responsibility." Not that Becky had any plans to move out. Expanding her business over the coming months was her priority.

"True." He added more coleslaw and potato salad to his plate. "Mum called this afternoon. Bella is settled at school, and reconnecting with friends who are a good influence."

"I'm glad." Joel had spent a lot of time with his sister during his three weeks in Australia.

Mom had also called this afternoon. As per their new normal, Mom didn't mention or acknowledge Joel's name. He didn't seem to exist in Mom's world. Hannah would keep praying, and continue therapy, to help her work through the complexities of her relationship with Mom.

They chatted over their meal and devoured the apple pie Hannah had baked for dessert.

Joel glanced at his watch. "The fireworks over the lake will start soon."

She looked out at the starry sky, not a cloud in sight to obscure their view of the annual Fourth of July fireworks.

Joel stood and held out his hand. "I have something to show you."

"Oh, okay." She threaded her fingers through his and stepped toward him.

He dropped down on one knee and pulled a small jewelry case out of his pocket.

"Joel." She gulped in a big breath, her heart racing like a shooting star in the sky.

He snagged her gaze, his beautiful blue eyes bright and overflowing with joy. "I called your father a few days ago, and he gave us his blessing."

She nodded, emotion choking her throat, and words elusive. It was happening. It was really happening.

"Hannah, I love you with my whole heart. With everything I have. In January, when I left Australia looking for a new start, I'd no idea I'd soon be meeting the woman I believe God chose for me."

Her eyes misted, his words a welcome and soothing balm that warmed her tender heart. "I love you." She was loved. Loved by Jesus and loved by Joel.

He opened the box, revealing a stunning round ruby set with diamonds in a white gold ring.

"It's gorgeous." She breathed in and out, holding his hand tight.

"Hannah Gilbertson, my beautiful and amazing girl, will you marry me?"

"Yes, yes." She leapt into his arms, excitement overflowing inside her.

He pulled back. "Haven't you forgotten something?"

"Oh, the ring." How could she forget the ring?

He cradled her left hand and slid the ring on her finger. A perfect fit.

"Joel, it's beautiful." She held out her hand, admiring the sparkling ruby from different angles.

The fireworks erupted, shooting red and blue streaks into the inky night sky. He circled his arm around her shoulders, joining her in watching the sky explode in an orchestrated display of spectacular colors.

She snuggled closer. "Happy Fourth of July." Her smile felt wider and deeper than the huge body of water in Lake Wainscott. "A night to remember and treasure."

"Yes." He dropped a sweet kiss on her lips, his love and commitment undeniable.

She could travel the globe and never find another man like Joel. She was blessed, and she looked forward to their future together.

AUTHOR'S NOTE

Thank you for reading *Never Find Another You*. I hope you enjoyed Joel and Hannah's romance story.

Never Find Another You is Book 1 in *Trinity Lakes Romance* multi-author contemporary Christian romance series. I was excited to have the opportunity to work with a wonderful group of authors to create the Trinity Lakes fictional story world. The books in the series are connected by the setting and characters who crossover between stories.

Please consider writing a review and sharing your thoughts on my book with other readers. I appreciate every review I receive for my stories. Reader reviews can help other readers find books that they'll enjoy reading.

ACKNOWLEDGMENTS

For my husband and young adult children who provided the support I needed to finish this book on time. Life happens and, like the characters in our books, obstacles can be thrown in our path that we need to overcome to reach The End.

A big thank you to the Trinity Lakes Romance author group who provided invaluable input on early drafts that assisted me in strengthening the story. Writing the first book in a new series presents unique challenges. Creating a shared story world that provides opportunities for future stories in the series is a team effort. I especially want to thank Meredith Resce, Lisa Renee, and Sara Beth Williams for their insightful critiques.

Thank you to Jen Richards for reading my messy first draft and pointing out issues I needed to address. I appreciate my family and friends, and my newsletter reader friends, who have provided prayers and support. To God be the glory.

Many thanks to my editor, Iola Goulton.

ABOUT THE AUTHOR

A fun loving Aussie girl at heart, Narelle Atkins was born and raised on the beautiful northern beaches in Sydney, Australia. She has settled in Canberra with her husband and children. A lifelong romance reader, she found the perfect genre to write when she discovered inspirational romance. Narelle's contemporary stories of faith and romance are set in Australia and international locations. To find out more visit her at Narelle-Atkins.com

Narelle also invites you to join her author newsletter list. Her newsletter subscribers are the first readers to see cover reveals and hear bookish news from Narelle.

OTHER TITLES BY NARELLE ATKINS

Sydney Sweethearts Series

Book 1 - Her Tycoon Hero

Book 2 - Winning Julia's Heart

(previously titled Winning Over the Heiress)

Book 3 - Seaside Proposal

Book 3.5 - Seaside Christmas novella

A Tuscan Legacy Series

Solo Tu: Only You (A Tuscan Legacy, Book 7)

Easter in Gilead

Her Cowboy Blind Date

Sapphire Bay Series

His Perfect Catch (novella)

A standalone novella and spinoff story from *Seaside Proposal* set in Sapphire Bay.